Did she have a choice?

"What would I have to do, exactly?" She stalled for time. "Attend one party, that is all..." she prompted, as though she was considering his proposition.

"Yes. And be nice to me, act as though we are in love," he drawled cynically, and before she could respond he had hauled her into his arms, her own arms pinned to her body.

At the touch of his hard body pressed against her own, her consideration flew out of the window. "I'm not that good an actress," she spat, her hands clenching at her sides in frustration, itching to slap his arrogant face.

"I'll teach you."

JACQUELINE BAIRD began writing as a hobby when her family objected to the smell of her oil painting! She immediately became hooked on the romance genre. Jacqueline loves traveling and worked her way around the world from Europe to the Americas and Australia, returning to marry her teenage sweetheart. The couple now live in Ponteland, Northumbria, with their two teenage sons. She enjoys playing badminton, and spends most weekends with husband Jim, sailing on the Derwent Reservoir.

Books by Jacqueline Baird

HARLEQUIN PRESENTS
1079—DARK DESIRING
1359—SHATTERED TRUST
1431—PASSIONATE BETRAYAL
1558—DISHONOURABLE PROPOSAL
1627—GUILTY PASSION

JACQUELINE BAIRD

Master of Passion

Harlequin Books

TORONTO • NEW YORK • LONDON
AMSTERDAM • PARIS • SYDNEY • HAMBURG
STOCKHOLM • ATHENS • TOKYO • MILAN
MADRID • WARSAW • BUDAPEST • AUCKLAND

ISBN 0-373-11683-7

MASTER OF PASSION

Copyright © 1993 by Jacqueline Baird.

Printed in U.S.A.

CHAPTER ONE

PARISA stealthily wriggled her slender body through the bathroom window, feet first. The window-ledge dug into her flat stomach as she felt around with one foot for the security of the bathroom floor.

Damn! she swore under her breath as water seeped into one trainer. She would kill her friend Moya, if she ever got her foot out of the toilet bowl and herself out of this escapade in one piece.

She must have been off her trolley to agree with Moya's hare-brained scheme to burgle a third-floor apartment in the heart of Mayfair. So what if her friend was being blackmailed? The stupid girl should have had more sense than to pose for some Latin man on a beach in the south of France, wearing only a thong. When Moya's engagement was announced in *The Times* to the son of a high-court judge whose brother was a bishop, no less, the Latin rat had got in touch with her and demanded money.

With an inward sigh of relief, Parisa felt her feet finally find the floor, and she slipped into the dark room. She stood quietly, allowing her eyes to grow accustomed to the gloom and trying to get her bearings. Yesterday, in the cool grey light of a February morning, the plan had seemed simple. Moya had arranged to meet the Italian this morning at his apartment, supposedly to negotiate the return of the photographs, and then she had contrived to leave the lavatory window open. Luckily the man hadn't noticed the open window before leaving for work. As manager of a London casino, there was no fear of him being at home on a Friday evening.

So far everything had gone according to plan. All Parisa had to do was walk across the hall to the sitting-room, and, according to Moya, locked in a drawer of a leather-topped desk were the incriminating photographs. Moya had watched the man put them there that very morning while fearfully promising to pay him the following day. So why now, ten o'clock at night and pitch-black outside, did Parisa have very grave doubts?

Still, the place seemed empty, she told herself reassuringly, and as her eyes grew accustomed to the dark she could see the outline of a door on the far wall. She stepped forward, and froze in horror.

A stream of light beamed across the bathroom from a partially open door at her side. She had almost walked into it. She swore violently under her breath, but the voices she heard were all too audible... Heart pounding with fear, she cowered behind the half-open door. On the opposite wall was a mirror, and in it she saw the reflection of a man. His back was towards her, but the woman standing to one side of him, her arms outstretched, was instantly recognisable to Parisa. It was Margot Mey, a stunning petite redhead and a famous, if not infamous, cabaret singer.

God! What a mess. Parisa's mouth was dry with fear. She was sure she would be discovered any second. She did not dare move a muscle.

'I assure you, Margot, I intended calling you tomorrow, but tonight I had and still have business to attend to.'

The deep, slightly accented voice sent a shiver of horror down Parisa's spine. So this was the 'sleazy little slimeball', to quote her friend. She might have guessed Moya, in her near frantic state, would get it all wrong. There was nothing small about the man. He must be well over six feet—about six-four, she guessed—and, judging by the breadth of his back, big with it, and he certainly wasn't at any casino, but standing in the bedroom...

'Luc, darling, don't be angry.' Two slender hands curved around the back of the man's neck. 'I couldn't wait to see you. It's been so long; I've missed you.'

Parisa could feel the colour flood up her face. Luc—she had heard that name before, but it couldn't be. She shook her head, dismissing the thought, but felt the sweat break out on her brow beneath the thick black Balaclava hat she had pulled over her fine platinum hair. She had to get out of here, and quick. The couple were kissing, and it was obviously only a matter of time before they fell on the bed behind them. But to her amazement the man deftly removed the clinging hands from his neck and stepped back.

'Not tonight, Margot. I told you I'm busy. I'll see you home,' he said coolly.

'But Luc...'

'No.'

Parisa almost felt sorry for the woman, her beautiful face flushed with anger at the man's arrogant rejection, but the fury was quickly masked behind a sensuous smile. 'Turned down by the master of passion himself!' she husked throatily. 'Why, Luc? You know how good we can be, and it's been so long.'

Parisa just managed to stifle a snort of disgust. 'Master of passion'—what a joke! Master of pornography, more like. Couldn't the woman see what a jerk the chap was?

'Maybe, but not at the moment. I will make it up to you tomorrow, I promise. But now you must leave.'

'Does that mean you've reconsidered and will take me to Italy next week for your mother's party? After all, Luc darling, we have been together for almost a year. A very wonderful year,' she breathed throatily.

Parisa almost choked. Had the woman no pride?

'Margot, let's get one thing straight. There is no way I can introduce you to my mother, and you know that. Your affairs have been legion and very public,' he chuckled. 'The whole of Italy, including my mother, saw the picture of you dancing naked on the table in the best restaurant in Rome, with a member of the government as your companion.'

'You mean I am good enough to sleep with, but not to marry,' the woman cut in bitterly.

'Be realistic. We have had an excellent arrangement, you and I.' The man's hand curved coaxingly around the woman's shoulder. 'Don't spoil it by asking more. Now, you really must go. As a matter of interest, how did you know where to find me?' His voice faded as, to Parisa's relief, he urged the woman towards the bedroom door. But for a second Parisa had the uneasy feeling that his voice was familiar.

'Your arrival was in the newspaper and I knew you had bought the casino, so when you weren't at the usual place I checked with the casino, and they gave me the address of...'

Parisa could hear no more, but her blood boiled with anger. The swine must have blackmailed a hell of a lot of women if he could afford to buy one of the biggest private casinos in London. She heard the door shut, and then the sound of yet another door closing told her they were gone.

Carefully she wiped her sweaty palms down over her slim hips. The black leotard she was wearing absorbed some of the moisture. That was a close shave, she thought, breathing deeply until slowly her heartbeat returned to something like normal. Then, swiftly and silently, she moved out of the bathroom and into the hall.

The excitement that had sent her adrenalin sky-high as she had climbed up the fire-escape had now turned to a deep fear, bordering on panic. She must have been *mad*! she told herself, but resolutely she crossed the hall, opened yet another door and found herself in a large, gloomy room. She did not dare turn on the light, but carefully withdrew a torch from the pouch on the wide leather belt circling her waist. She switched it on. Yes, there was the desk. Swiftly crossing the room, she tried the first drawer. It was locked. Digging once more into the pouch at her waist, she found a penknife. Her full lips quirked in a brief smile. If the scout troop could see her now!

Bending over the desk, she inserted the knife between the wood and the lock, and wriggled it around. Nothing happened. It looked easy enough on the movies, she thought with exasperation, and, leaning lower, she began jabbing at the stubborn lock. A sharp crack and she'd done it!

There was the packet of photographs. Quickly she took them out and, straightening, she ran the torch over the snaps. Yes, it was Moya all right. Considering some people bathed completely naked in the south of France, they were hardly pornographic. If Moya had been marrying into any other family, they would not have caused a ripple. Parisa smiled in satisfaction. Mission accomplished! She turned and walked straight into a large male body.

'Got you.'

She did not know what had hit her. Before she could cry out a strong-muscled arm had caught her around the waist, and flung her down on the floor. Parisa opened her mouth to scream when her attacker landed heavily on top of her, knocking the air out of her lungs so that the scream came out as a high-pitched squeak. She was enveloped in the musky scent of a warm male body. Parisa, stunned for a moment, made no attempt to escape. Still dazed, she realised she was flat on her back on the floor with what felt like a ton weight sitting on top of her. Her wrists were jerked above her head and pinned to the floor, and she saw an arm raised to strike her.

'Get off me, you great brute!' she screamed, finally finding her voice. 'Or I'll call the police.' She was so furious that she never realised the incongruity of her remark, and with all the breath knocked out of her she was not in much of a condition to fight. But she did her best, bucking wildly beneath the hard body trapping her.

The hand that she had thought was about to strike her roughly pulled the black Balaclava from her head. Her platinum hair fell down in wild disarray as a large hand cupped her chin.

'Well, well, what have we here?'

He sounded like a ham actor in a B movie, Parisa thought irrelevantly, but quickly lost her sense of humour, suddenly aware of her appalling predicament. His heavy thighs gripped her waist. He was bent over her, his other hand firmly clasping her wrists. She was helpless. She felt the warmth of his breath on her face, and by the dim light of her torch, which was now lying on the floor, she saw the man's face for the first time...

'You!' she squeaked. 'I might have known.' He was older, but there was no mistaking the black, winged eyebrows, the hard line of his jaw, and the ruthless black eyes.

'*Dio*. Parisa.'

She stared, mesmerised as his handsome face came closer. Then everything went dark as his mouth crushed down on hers. He kissed her with a savage, angry passion—not a kiss, a defilement. Her head began to swim; she was going to pass out if she did not breathe soon.

Then a blinding light flashed in her eyes. The man's head jerked up, but he did not set her free. Dazed, Parisa moved her head to one side and saw a pair of elegantly shod feet, a slender, very feminine ankle.

'Really, Luc, surely you could have waited until you got to the bedroom?'

'Tina. You've arrived.' A deep, rasping voice echoed in Parisa's stunned mind.

'At the wrong moment, obviously.' The light laugh was followed by a shocked cry. 'My God! Parisa Belmont, after all this time! I never knew you two had kept in touch, but I'm delighted. I always thought you would make a great couple.'

From flat on her back on the floor, Parisa looked up into the grinning face of Tina Franco, a girl who had briefly attended the same boarding-school as herself. Parisa muttered a polite, 'Good evening, Tina.' Had she really said that? What an idiot. It was all just too much. The whole fiasco bore all the hallmarks of a French farce.

She closed her eyes. This was a nightmare; it had to be. But the weight of the man straddling her was very real; the slight, lingering trace of his cologne teased her nostrils. Suddenly her eyes flew open. There was no mistaking the hard masculine length of him pressing into her stomach. The filthy swine was fully aroused...

'Let me up,' she whispered fiercely, her pale face scarlet with embarrassment. As if he had just realised the intimate position they were in, he immediately jumped to his feet. Keeping his back to the latest arrival, he stretched out a hand to help Parisa to her feet. Not letting go of her hand, he slowly turned to face Tina.

'Sorry about that, cousin, but you did promise to call earlier.'

'Yes, well, Gino and I decided to eat first. We weren't sure if the apartment was near a restaurant. He's waiting downstairs in the taxi; we are flying back to Italy tonight.' And, holding out a black briefcase, she added, 'All the papers you wanted are in there. I have to dash!' Turning a brilliant smile on Parisa, she concluded with, 'It is great to see you again. I'm sorry I haven't time to chat, but you must come to the party on Tuesday. Luc's mother will be delighted to meet you. *Ciao.*' And she was gone.

The silence was deafening. Parisa tried to ease her hand from Luc's, but, without a word, he tightened his grasp and half dragged her across the room to a large hide sofa, and with a jerk of her hand he pushed her down. 'Sit down.'

She had no choice but to obey. Nervously she rubbed her cramped fingers. If she had had the slightest suspicion that the man Moya had been involved with was

Luca Di Maggi—Luc, to his friends—she would have run a mile. She had met the man once, at the tender age of fourteen, and she had hoped never to see him again.

'So, Parisa Belmont—or should I say Lady Parisa Hardcourt-Belmont?' His mocking drawl grated on her shredded nerves. 'We meet again, and it is obvious age has not taught you any discretion. Perhaps you could explain what you think you are doing, dressed up like a cat burglar, and breaking into this apartment.'

He was towering over her, and for the first time that evening she got a really good look at him, a feeling of helplessness washing over her as she stared up at him. Huge and elegant, his dark jacket taut over his broad shoulders, his white silk shirt open at the throat, revealing the firm tanned flesh beneath, the slight dark shadowing of body hair clearly visible. He was powerful, all male and, as her wary blue eyes met his, absolutely furious.

'If you are so desperate for money I would have thought a woman of your obvious charms could have tried the oldest profession, before resorting to stealing,' he said cynically, his dark eyes raking her slender frame with a blatant sexual thoroughness that left her feeling as if he had stripped her naked.

She swallowed nervously, looking away, and her glance fell on the packet of photographs lying where she had dropped them on the carpet. The sight of them reminded her why she was in this mess, and grim determination stiffened her spine. She sat up straight, lifting her head to stare into the harsh face of her adversary.

'It is not money *I* am after. That is surely your game, Luc. But you tried to blackmail the wrong girl when you picked on Moya. She is a friend of mine.' She did not bother to mask the derision in her brilliant blue eyes. It was this man who was outside the law, not her, she told herself firmly. 'As for breaking in——'

'I left the door open for a moment.' He said the words softly, as though he was talking to himself, and for a second Parisa caught a puzzled look in his dark eyes as his gaze swung searchingly around the room. 'You walked in.' He moved towards the desk, opened the drawer, then noticed the photographs on the floor and, bending down, picked them up.

She did not bother to correct him. There was no need for him to know she had seen him with his mistress. Parisa watched him flick through the photographs, his sensuous mouth curving in a knowing smile.

'You came for these?' he queried, turning towards her.

The swine knew damn well she had. 'Of course.' She rose to her feet and bravely walked across to Luc. 'And as for paying thousands for them, you can go whistle.' She reached out and caught one end of the packet, but Luc quickly grasped her wrist and, by the simple expedient of tightening his grip, forced her to let go.

'Not so fast, Parisa. You think I am blackmailing this girl.' He shook the packet in front of her. 'So you decided to break into this apartment and steal the evidence. Have I got that right?'

'Don't try to play the innocent with me, Luc Di Maggi. I know all about your little game. To supplement your income from the casino you blackmail defenceless young women,' she jeered.

'The casino—you know about that?'

What was the matter with the man? Did he really think he could fool her with all these questions? 'Either you give me those photographs or I call the police,' she bluffed. The touch of his hand on her wrist, the closeness of his large frame, was having a very odd effect on her overstrung nerves. She had to get out of here, and quick. Apart from anything else, she did not have a great deal of confidence in Moya. The girl was terrified, and it would not take much to push Moya over the edge and make her drive off if Parisa was much longer.

Luc's deep voice broke the lengthening silence. 'The police, Parisa? You surprise me. I thought you were more intelligent.'

'Blackmail is a major crime,' she snapped.

'But, my dear Parisa, by the time the police arrive I will have burnt the evidence, and all they will find is a young woman dressed for robbery.' His dark eyes skated over her, his lips tilting in a sensual smile as his eyes lingered on her full breasts.

Suddenly she realised what a sight she must look. The black leotard and black tights clung to every curve of her slender body like a second skin. Defensively she folded her arms over her chest, at a loss for words. If he did burn the evidence Moya's problem would be solved, but hers would only just be starting.

'Yes, *cara*.' He watched the changing emotions flickering across her lovely face. 'Instead they will see you, your knife and my broken desk. With the addition of a bundle of money, I think I can safely say you will end up serving a rather long gaol sentence.'

His scenario was all too easy to believe, Parisa realised with a sinking heart, and her brief burst of confidence dwindled to nothing. Instead she stared up into a pair of cold black eyes, fearful of what would come next.

'However I'll make a deal with you. If you are agreeable, I will guarantee that your friend receives the photographs and negatives very soon, and in complete secrecy.'

'A deal.' She did not trust him. How could she? He was a crook, but she had to hear him out. 'What kind of deal?' she demanded, managing to sound much more in control than she felt.

Casually he strolled across the room and, placing the vital package in the drawer of a long mahogany sideboard, he picked up a bottle of whisky from a silver tray placed on top, and poured a generous measure of liquid into a crystal tumbler. 'Join me in a drink and I will explain.' His dark head turned towards her. 'Whisky, or perhaps brandy would be better. You look a little shocked.'

Shocked did not begin to describe Parisa's feelings, and there was no way she was going to share a drink with the man. 'Nothing for me, thank you,' she refused. 'Just get on with it.'

'Such impatience,' he mocked, and in a few lithe strides he crossed the room and sprawled his large frame in the chair opposite. He took a sip of the amber liquid, his dark eyes fixed on her with a narrow-eyed scrutiny, as if he was coming to some conclusion in his own mind. 'Yes,' he murmured almost to himself. 'Well, Parisa, it is quite simple. As Tina mentioned when she so rudely interrupted us, I have to go to my mother's birthday party in Italy on Tuesday.'

'I'm surprised you have a mother,' she muttered.

'Crude, Parisa...'

'Yes, well get on with it.'

'My mother is seventy, but sadly not in the best of health, and it is her dearest wish to see me married. I have no desire to put my head in that particular noose, but for my mother's peace of mind I don't mind pretending, and that's where you come in.'

Parisa looked at him suspiciously; she did not think she liked the sound of this at all. Her blue eyes lingered on his face. He was a very handsome man. Thick dark hair fell in a slight wave across his broad forehead. His dark eyes were half closed, disguising his expression behind thick, curling lashes. His mouth was wide, the bottom lip slightly fuller than the top, his chin square and hard. His typical Roman nose gave an added ruggedness to features that would otherwise have been classically handsome.

'How?' she asked warily.

'You come to Italy and act as my fiancée for a couple of days, and your friend gets her photographs back. I think my mother will be suitably impressed with an English Lady as a prospective daughter-in-law, and it will get her off my back for a while.'

Parisa saw it all, of course. His mistress had begged to go with him earlier, and he had bluntly turned her down. Parisa never used her title, but she was quite used to other people using it when trying to impress. But could she stomach a couple of days in the company of a crook? And at the moment, virtually his prisoner, did she have a choice?

'What would I have to do, exactly?' She stalled for time. Luc placed his glass on a nearby table and, rising, moved to stand in front of her, much too close for her liking. She raised her head, his dark presence intimidating her. 'Attend one party, that is all…' she prompted, as though she was considering his proposition.

'Yes. And be nice to me, act as though we are in love,' he drawled cynically, and before she could respond he had hauled her into his arms, her own arms pinned to her body.

At the touch of his hard body pressed against her own, her consideration flew out of the window. 'I'm not that good an actress,' she spat, her hands clenching at her sides in frustration, itching to slap his arrogant face, but unable to move.

'I'll teach you,' he mocked, correctly reading the anger in her eyes, and amused by it.

'Why, you arrogant swine!' she fumed, but the rest of her words were swallowed as his dark head swooped down, his mouth capturing hers. She twisted sharply, trying to break free of his hold, but as his mouth continued to ravage hers she felt her anger fading, and the unexpected coil of desire uncurling in her stomach. No! she told herself, but as his lips softened on hers, and somehow his tongue found a way between her teeth, her pulse leapt alarmingly.

She was aware of the hard muscular chest pressed against her breasts, and to her horror she could feel her nipples begin to tighten in an aching response. She vaguely heard a moan—Luc or herself, she was not sure.

The moist heat of his mouth burnt as he broke the kiss and trailed kisses to the pulse beating madly in her neck. His tongue licked lightly, almost soothingly; then he was holding her away from him.

'That will do for starters,' he said coolly. 'And you are quite wrong, Parisa. If that kiss is anything to go by, you have lost none of your acting talent.'

She stared up at him, her blue eyes dazed by the force of her own emotional response. He was smiling a cold, cynical smile, as though the last couple of minutes had never happened. Parisa despised him, but she despised herself more. To allow a man of his character to arouse her sexuality was so humiliating. There was no way she was going to Italy with him. Moya would have to sort the mess out herself. Parisa no longer dared. Her one thought was how to get out of the apartment, away from this man.

'Don't look so shocked, *cara*, you won't have to perform too often.'

'Yes, well, all right,' she said with commendable calm, considering that her legs were trembling. Her mind was racing, and she knew what she had to do. 'I think I will have that drink now, and we can discuss the details, but first I must visit the bathroom.'

'Good girl, I knew you would see it my way. After all, it is to our mutual benefit.' He smiled.

Parisa forced a smile in response, turned, and almost made a mistake by heading straight for the bathroom. She swung back around. 'Where is the bathroom?' she asked with pseudo innocence.

'Straight across the hall. I'll show you.' And with a hand at her back he urged her into the hall, and gestured with his other hand to the bathroom door. 'I will have the champagne waiting to celebrate our deal,' he said silkily, while making sure he stood between Parisa, the front door and escape.

'How lovely.' The swine was in for a shock, she thought gleefully.

In seconds she was in the bathroom, back out of the window, and down the fire-escape. She heaved a sigh of relief at the sight of Moya's familiar blue Fiat still waiting. Running along the back lane, she opened the passenger door and jumped in.

'Drive quickly.'

'Did you get them?' Moya demanded urgently.

'Not now, Moya, hurry!' And with a grinding of gears the car shot forward.

Half an hour later, seated in a comfortable armchair in Moya's apartment in Kensington, a glass of brandy in her hand, Parisa took a large gulp of the fiery liquid, and slowly began to relax.

'For God's sake, Parisa, don't keep me in suspense. I can't bear it. Have you got the photographs?'

Parisa looked at her friend sitting opposite. Moya was medium height with long chestnut hair, big brown eyes, and a figure that rivalled Marilyn Monroe's. Yet perched on the edge of the chair, an apprehensive expression marring her beautiful face, and dark shadows under her eyes, she looked positively haggard.

'I'm sorry, Moya. It was a total flop.'

'But how? All you had to do was climb in and get them. You're a sports mistress, for heaven's sake!' she wailed. 'You were my last hope.'

'Oh, I got in all right. Unfortunately, contrary to your information, the place was not empty. Your Italian was there, and, by the way——' Parisa grimaced '—I would hardly have called the man small. He knocked me down with no trouble at all.'

'Oh, my God!'

'Exactly! Prayers are all you have left, my friend...' Parisa said bluntly. 'There is no way I am having anything more to do with this. I was crazy to agree in the first place, and how come you told me his name was Luigi something or other? The man is called Luca Di Maggi, and if I had known that I wouldn't have gone within ten miles of his apartment.'

'Luigi, Luca, what's the difference?' Moya responded, the agitation evident in her tone. 'You still haven't told me what happened. He must have said something.'

In a few short sentences Parisa described the events of the evening, leaving out the part about his mistress. She lifted a finger to her slightly swollen lips, the memory of his kisses oddly disturbing. 'Anyway, there I was on the carpet, imagining he was going to kill me, when this woman walked in. Do you remember Tina Franco?'

'That mysterious Italian girl from school, the one whose family we thought belonged to the Mafia... But what are we reminiscing for when my life is——?'

Parisa cut in, 'She's a cousin of his. Anyway, she recognised me, and thought we were a couple. Seemingly the man's mother is having a birthday party next week, and he had the gall to suggest that if I went to Italy with him and acted as his fiancée he would give me the photographs.'

'You'll have to go, Parisa. Please... My whole future is at stake here. You've got to help me. I couldn't bear to lose Simon, and I will, I know I will, if those photographs are ever published...'

'No, Moya. I would do a lot for you. But I am not going anywhere with Di Maggi, and I honestly can't understand how you got mixed up with him. I think your best bet is to explain everything to Simon. He loves you; he will forgive you one lover, surely.'

'Lover!' Moya screeched. 'Never...! I met the man with a crowd of friends at the casino. Then last summer I went on holiday to Nice with the same crowd, and he happened to be there. We were all on the beach and he took those photographs. I only went out with him once when I got back from holiday, and he was like an octopus, so I chased him. I'm still a virgin,' she ended tremulously.

'Ah. Well, then...you've nothing to worry about. Tell Simon the truth and forget about the crook.'

'I can't, Parisa. He worships me, and I love him. If those pictures ever appear in a newspaper it would destroy everything. His family would disown me. So, you see, you must help me.' She leant forward, clutching Parisa's arm. 'You could do it, Parisa. You're on half-term holiday from school. A call to your housekeeper, extending your stay—tell her we're going shopping for the bridesmaid's dress on Monday. Please! I have no one else to turn to.'

Parisa almost succumbed to her friend's pleading, until she had a vivid mental image of the man concerned lying on top of her, his lips ravaging hers. A shudder danced down her spine and she sat up stiffly in the low chair.

'No, Moya, I'm sorry. In the morning I'm going to get the first train back home before that man has a chance to catch up with me. He knows your address, and I'm not taking any chances. Talk to Simon. He loves you; he will understand. Or call the police. Now I'm going to bed.' She stood up.

'Please, Parisa,' Moya begged. 'My future happiness is at stake.' Her bottom lip trembled. 'We've always helped each other before. Remember the time you wanted to go to the pop concert? You climbed out of the dormitory window, down the oak tree. I covered for you when Miss Cliff checked the dorm, and stayed up half the night to drag you back in.'

Parisa felt terribly guilty, letting Moya down, but she couldn't explain the fear she felt in Luc Di Maggi's presence. Not without explaining about a summer day ten years ago, and she had told no one—not even Moya— what had happened. She had made a fool of Luc Di Maggi, and he was not the type of man to forgive easily. She just knew instinctively that to get tangled up with the man would do her nothing but harm... 'Sorry,' she muttered, heading for the door.

'OK, Parisa, if you can't, you can't,' Moya said sadly. 'I suppose I will have to sleep with the man, although the very thought makes my flesh crawl.'

'What!' Parisa cried, spinning on her heel to face her friend.

'Well, he did say cash or kind, and as neither you nor I have the cash...' Moya's anguished words trailed off, her brown eyes desolate.

Parisa was hit with a host of conflicting emotions. That the swine could blackmail women into his bed was beyond belief, and she hated the thought of Moya being one of them. She glanced at her friend. Moya looked completely crushed, and yet some devil deep inside Parisa whispered that Luc Di Maggi was far too attractive, too much male. He was more likely to be fighting women off than having to blackmail them into his bed. He must really want Moya badly—either that or he was a sex maniac! Neither thought gave Parisa any comfort.

'If you won't help me I have no choice. I couldn't bare to see the disgust in Simon's eyes if he ever saw those pictures. I just couldn't live without Simon. Please, Parisa.'

'Let's sleep on it, Moya. Things always look better in the morning.'

CHAPTER TWO

WEARILY Parisa stripped off her clothes, and stepped into the shower. She turned the water to hot and stood under the refreshing spray. God! What a night. But then she should have known. On the rare occasions she gave in to the reckless side of her nature it invariably ended in a fiasco, and becoming a cat burglar had not been a good idea. Parisa loved Moya dearly, but the girl was virtually incapable of looking after herself. They had met as fourteen-year-olds at Brenlodge School for Girls. Parisa had just lost her parents in, of all things, a hot-air balloon attempt at crossing the Atlantic. Moya's mother had recently died in a car crash. Her father was a self-made man who worked all the hours God sent and had little time for his daughter, and so had sent the girl to boarding-school. Parisa and Moya had become firm friends, Moya spending most of the school holidays with Parisa at her home, Hardcourt Manor, as her own father was rarely at their Norfolk home.

When Parisa had gone to university and then into teaching at a private school in Battle near her home, they had still kept in touch. In fact it was when Moya had spent last Christmas with Parisa that she had met Simon and fallen in love at first sight. His father had just bought the estate adjacent to Parisa's home.

Parisa sighed. She felt in some way responsible for her friend, but what she could do about it she hadn't a clue. Turning off the tap, she stepped out of the shower, took a large towel off the heated rail, and briskly rubbed herself dry. What she would like to do was murder Luc Di Maggi, but it wasn't really an option, she told herself wryly. She was tired, her head ached, and all she wanted was sleep. She walked into the bedroom, dropped the towel to the floor, and climbed, naked, into bed, but sleep was elusive.

Every time she closed her eyes the image of Luc Di Maggi appeared in her mind. She had not thought about him in years, but tonight, seeing him and Tina again, had brought it all back.

At fourteen she had been exactly the same as she was now. Five feet nine, platinum, almost silver hair, and fully developed. She had loved school and excelled at sports, and, looking back, she could see that was probably why Tina had sought her out. Tina had been eighteen and in her last term at school. One Saturday morning she had cornered the much younger Parisa and asked her if she would do her a favour. Seemingly her boyfriend was arriving to see her that day, but her cousin was coming with him as a chaperon, and would Parisa make up the foursome to distract the cousin?

Parisa had been so naïve and slightly in awe of a sixth-former actually wanting to speak to her that she had agreed to everything. She had meekly allowed Tina to dress her up in one of her skirts, which might have been respectable on her five-foot-two frame, but was indecently short on Parisa. The scoop-necked blouse had not been much better. With the addition of make-up, by the time Tina had finished Parisa easily looked eighteen.

Tina had coached her well. 'Just remember you are eighteen, in my class, and my good friend, if Luc asks. Flutter your eyelashes a bit and hang on to his every word and he'll be eating out of your hand. He's a sucker for leggy blondes; you'll have no trouble at all. By the way, you're captain of the rowing team and have the key to the boat-house, don't you?'

Parisa quickly confirmed the fact, and Tina had said, 'Well, just for fun, I want you to show Luc the boats and accidentally lock him in for a while.'

But it had not quite worked out that way. Parisa had taken one look at the tall dark man and, even at her tender age, had known he was not the sort to play tricks on. At first everything went fine. In fact, walking along the river-bank, with Luc's hand cupping her elbow, she had found they had no trouble talking. He'd told her he was twenty-six years old, single, and looking. She had responded by telling him she was eighteen and looking. He had made her laugh, and she did not have to pretend to like him—she did. He was stunningly attractive and rather mysterious. She had asked him what he did for a living and he had replied by saying he had, 'fingers in many pies'.

As they neared the boat-house Tina had given her a dig in the back to remind her of the plan. Parisa had smiled up into Luc's face and asked with a flutter of her long lashes if he would like to see the boat she rowed in the four-women sculls. He had teasingly said, 'I would love to see your stroke any time, Parisa'. She had fought to keep the blush from her cheeks, and, turning her back to him, opened the door. She intended standing aside to let him go first, but he had forestalled her, by taking her arm and urging her inside.

It was then that Tina had turned the key, locking them both in. Luc had glanced curiously at the boats in the dim light from the one small window and then, to her utter amazement, had turned and taken her in his arms. It was the first time a man had kissed her, and she had been stunned.

His mouth had been firm but gentle, and Parisa had relaxed against his hard frame and given herself up to the wonderful sensations he aroused.

Parisa moved uncomfortably in the bed. Ten years on she could still remember every word he had spoken, every touch, and her body flooded with heat as she replayed the scene in her mind.

'*Dio*! But you're beautiful,' Luc had whispered, holding her slightly away from him. Parisa had thought Luc would be furious, but surprisingly he was not. In the gloom she'd seen the smile on his face as he'd murmured, 'I couldn't have planned it better myself,' and kissed her again.

She had not known what was happening. His tongue had pushed between her teeth; his hands had roamed caressingly up and down her spine. Then one hand had slipped up and over her high, pert breast, his fingers sliding down the front of her blouse. She was drowning in a million sensations. Her hands had fluttered to his shoulders and clung. Her heart had pounded, with fear mingled with an aching excitement.

His other hand had eased up the hem of her skirt, and when she felt the touch of his long fingers on her naked thigh she had begun to tremble. It was only when he'd murmured huskily against her ear, 'Let's lie down— it's much better that way,' that she finally came to her senses and began to struggle.

Even now she could still recall how frightened and humiliated she had felt, Parisa thought wryly. She had kissed a few men since then, but none had created the same devastating effect as her first kiss. She thought she had forgotten, but seeing Luc tonight had brought it all back.

She had cried, 'No!' and tried to push him away. But he had held her tightly to him and angrily told her exactly what he thought of her.

'No! You dare to say that, after the way you have behaved all afternoon—flirting, asking for it. Feel what you've done to me.' And for the first time in her life she had felt the force of a hard, aroused male body against her slender form. She had panicked and managed to break free, and, to her utter humiliation, burst into tears.

At that point the boat-house door had swung open, and to Parisa's horror the sports mistress had walked in. Miss Shipley had taken one look at the couple and demanded to know what was going on.

Luc Di Maggi, totally in control, had charmingly explained that he was Tina's cousin and visiting for the day. Parisa had offered to show him the boats and

somehow the door had locked behind them. The reason
for Parisa's tears was that she was frightened of the dark.

Miss Shipley had demanded of Parisa, 'Is this true,
girl?' and she had quietly agreed. 'Well, no harm done,
I suppose, and you *are* a foreigner,' she had added as if
to say Luc knew no better. 'But a man of your age should
have more sense than to wander around with a fourteen-
year-old child. You should have asked your cousin Tina,
instead of bothering Lady Parisa Hardcourt-Belmont.'
The scorn in Miss Shipley's voice had been harsh and
obvious.

Luc Di Maggi had exclaimed, 'Fourteen!' His
handsome face had paled beneath his tan, his dark eyes
flashing incredulously to the tall, shapely Parisa.

Even now, Parisa thought, turning restlessly in her
bed, she was not sure if Miss Shipley had glossed over
the matter to save a young girl embarrassment, or, more
realistically, had not punished her because the following
day was the start of inter-school rowing championship
week, and Parisa was her star performer.

She yawned widely and pulled the blankets around her
chin. The past was over and not worth worrying about,
but she wasn't surprised Luc had ended up a crook. He
had lingered in her mind as a ruthless man.

Then she heard it... The soft but unmistakable sound
of Moya sobbing in the room next door. As she listened
to the pitiful sound, she knew she had no choice. She
would have to go with Luc to Italy. There was no way
she could let herself be responsible for the destruction
of Moya's happiness, when it was within her power to
prevent it.

Would it really be so terrible? A couple of days in
Italy with Luc Di Maggi? she asked herself. She was no
longer a scared young girl, but a mature woman of
twenty-four, with a responsible job. As for Di Maggi,
he was hardly likely to leap on her in his mother's house,
and why would he want to? He had a very beautiful
mistress—Margot Mey.

*   *   *

Sitting at the kitchen table the next morning, cradling a cup of strong coffee in her slender hands, Parisa studied her friend's swollen face and red-rimmed eyes. 'OK, Moya. I'll do it. Give me the man's telephone number and I'll call him.' She was almost suffocated in a bear-hug as soon as she spoke.

'You darling. I knew I could count on you,' Moya proclaimed, a watery smile lighting her wan face.

Extracting herself from Moya's arms, Parisa stood up and demanded, 'Give me the number, hmm?'

'I don't have the number, but it doesn't matter. Simon will be here soon.' Her eyes lit with love. 'We are going to buy the wedding rings. It will be no trouble to drop you off at Mayfair. We can tell Simon you're calling on a girlfriend. Then you can speak to the man, in person.' Her expression deadly serious, she added, 'And thank you, Parisa, you've saved my life. I couldn't bear to lose Simon; I love him so.'

Parisa hated the idea, but in the face of her friend's obvious relief she had not the heart to argue, and by nine-thirty a.m. was standing outside the entrance door of a familiar building.

With an unsteady hand she nervously jabbed at the bell marking the third-floor apartment, wishing she was anywhere in the world but here.

'Yes? Who is it?' a snarling voice demanded on the intercom.

Parisa zipped the jacket of her cream leather blouson tight to her throat, and, smoothing the soft hide of the matching, softly flared skirt with a shaking hand, she responded. 'Miss Belmont, Mr Di Maggi.'

'Parisa...' Her name was a bellow. 'Don't move... No. Come straight up.'

Tentatively she pushed the door and it swung open. She walked into the brightly lit hall and slowly began ascending the stairs. She had barely reached the first landing when Luc Di Maggi appeared. She stopped dead

as the full force of his virile masculinity hit her like a
punch in the stomach.

He looked as though he had just got out of bed: a
dark stubble covered his square jaw, a soft cotton shirt
flung across his broad shoulders was not yet fastened,
revealing a broad, muscular chest liberally covered in
black curling hair that narrowed to a single line over his
stomach and down to where a pair of well-washed jeans
hung low on narrow hips, the top snap unfastened. He
was barely decent... She swallowed hard, and before
she could speak he grabbed her arm in a grip of steel.

'What the hell did you think you were doing, Parisa?
Are you completely crazy? Climbing out of a window
and down a fire ladder in the middle of the night. You
could have broken your beautiful neck, you idiot...'

He was furiously angry; his black eyes bore down into
her surprised blue ones with an intensity that made her
shiver. He looked as if murder was not far from his mind.
'I'm perfectly all right. What's the matter, Luc, scared
you might have been arrested for murder, instead of
blackmail?' she sneered, determined he should know
from the beginning just what kind of low-life she considered him.

Luc's arm tightened for a second and then she was
free. His gaze narrowed on her beautiful but flushed face.
'No, Parisa, I'm not afraid of anything or anyone, but
you would be wise to guard your tongue around me.
There is only so much I will take from you, little lady.
Last night you took ten years off my life in ten minutes.'

Her blue eyes widened in astonishment. For a second
she could have sworn she saw genuine concern in the
depths of his dark eyes before his hooded lids dropped,
masking his expression.

'If you want to help your friend—and I imagine that
is why you are here—follow me...' he commanded.

Reluctantly Parisa followed him up the stairs, his
broad back just asking for a knife between the shoulder-
blades, she thought bitterly, but it did not stop her ad-

miring the tight round curve of his buttocks, or the long, sinewy legs. What was happening to her? She had never been plagued with erotic thoughts about a man's physique before. She was so lost in thought that she walked straight into Luc's back, pushing him through his own door.

'Such haste. I'm flattered.' He turned and, grinning broadly, swept her into his arms and swung her around and into his apartment, adding, 'Or are you terrified in case someone sees you with me, a notorious villain?'

Parisa, with her feet once more on the floor, shot him a vitriolic look. She was a tall girl and was not used to being literally swept off her feet by any man, and she had a nasty suspicion he was laughing at her. Mustering all her self-control, she retorted, 'Being engaged to you even for only two days would certainly not enhance any woman's reputation.'

'Ah, now we come to the reason for your unexpected visit. You are regretting your hasty departure last night, and want to accept my proposition, is that not so?' he asked cynically.

'More or less,' she muttered, hating to admit defeat.

'I'm sorry, I drank the champagne. We can discuss it over a coffee instead,' he drawled smoothly, adding, 'Follow me.'

If the pig told her once more to follow him she was going to walk out, Parisa vowed, but she did follow him into a sparkling kitchen, all stainless steel and tiles, with every gadget known to man.

'Sit down, Parisa, while I make the coffee.'

'Hadn't you better finish dressing first?' she asked coldly, sitting down on a black and chrome chair. It was difficult enough having to speak to the man without being confronted by acres of male flesh all the time.

'My apologies,' he offered facetiously, 'but I over-slept this morning, probably because I was up most of the night, worrying about a certain Lady Parisa...'

Liar. In his line of work it must be the norm to sleep in the morning. She stared down at the table. She would not respond to his sarcasm, even if she choked to death in the effort to hold back the words. Instead, through clenched teeth, she grated, 'Parisa will do fine.' Remember Moya, the wedding, be civil to the man, she told herself. Two days was not a lifetime. Think positive: a free trip to Italy can't be bad! God knew she certainly could not afford a holiday abroad on her own, and as for David, her boyfriend, a teacher like herself, but with a mother to support, his idea of a holiday was camping with the scouts. She frowned; she had forgotten David.

Parisa jumped when a large tanned hand placed a cup of coffee on the table in front of her. She lifted her head. Luc was sitting opposite her, one strong hand curved around a large mug of coffee, the other rubbing idly at his rough jaw.

'Parisa is a peculiar name; how did you acquire it?' he asked conversationally, before raising the mug to his lips and taking a deep drink of the steaming brew.

Her eyes strayed to the long column of his throat, its muscles moving beneath the tanned flesh as he swallowed. Hastily she took a drink of her own coffee before answering. 'My parents once went on an archaeological dig in what was Persia, and fell in love with the name Parisa. Apparently it is Persian for angelic-looking.'

'Very appropriate; you are an exquisitely beautiful woman, but then you were a beautiful child.'

Parisa could feel the colour washing up her throat at his extravagant compliment and avoided looking at him. Instead she fixed her gaze somewhere over his left shoulder, willing the colour to subside.

'Blushing...you surprise me, Parisa.' His hand reached out, and he ran one long finger down her hot cheek. 'I remember you at eighteen. No, fourteen, wasn't it?' he prompted silkily.

His touch was like a burning brand on her cheek. She flinched, glancing warily at his handsome face. He was smiling, but the smile did not reach his eyes. His dark gaze was hard on her flushed face. 'So, what of it?' she murmured stupidly.

'You may have been a liar, but you were also a passionate little thing. Some things never change.'

'That is unfair: it was your cousin Tina who talked me into it,' she responded angrily. She would not be called a liar by a crook. As for her passionate nature, she didn't have one. It was only around Luc that her emotions became explosive. Why? She had no idea.

'Maybe, but it wasn't Tina who flashed her big blue eyes at me, or rubbed suggestively against me. It was you, Parisa, which is why I am surprised you still blush. There must have been a lot of men in your life by now, judging by the passionate way you responded at such an early age.'

'Why, you insulting——' Her temper flared.

Luc, to her astonishment, grinned wickedly. 'Come on, Parisa, I was only teasing, and you do rise to the bait so beautifully.'

'Yes, well, enough about the past.' She had to get the conversation back to Moya.

'I like recalling old times,' Luc cut in. 'Especially unique events. A twenty-six-year-old man caught by the teacher kissing a schoolgirl! The most embarrassing moment of my life. I have always been curious to know what happened to you. The teacher must have punished you.'

'No. No, she didn't.' Parisa drained her cup, finding it was not so painful to look back down the years. In fact, her lips twitched in the semblance of a smile. It was quite funny, really...

'A young girl, in her charge. Come on, she must have said something. I was furious at being fooled by a child, but I always felt a little guilty imagining you confined to the classroom for the rest of the term, or deprived privileges.'

'Quite the opposite.' Parisa grinned. That he had felt guilty about the incident was pleasing and she did not question why. 'You see, I was Miss Shipley's star oarswoman, and the inter-school championships started that week. She was taking no chances on reporting me to the head and having her best performer grounded.'

'I didn't realise you actually could row. I thought that was just a ruse.'

'Row? I made the Olympic team when I was at university,' she said proudly, quite forgetting to whom she was talking. 'I was UK champion in the single sculls when I was nineteen.'

'Did you win anything at the Olympics?'

'No.' She sighed: it was her one regret in life. 'I didn't actually get to row,' she said honestly, a far-away look hazing her lovely eyes.

'Let me guess: you sneaked out of the Olympic village after curfew, and were grounded.'

Luc smiled encouragingly across the table, and she found herself telling him the truth. 'Not exactly. I made friends with Jan, a Dutchman, who was a pole vaulter. It was something I had always fancied having a go at. Anyway, he let me try his pole. Unfortunately I fell badly and broke my leg.'

To her astonishment he threw his dark head back and howled with laughter. What was so funny? she thought belligerently, the friendly atmosphere of the past few minutes vanishing as she felt her anger rise. She had been devastated at the time, and this oaf was laughing at her. 'It wasn't funny. I was absolutely gutted.'

'No, no, of course not,' Luc spluttered, fighting to contain his amusement. 'And your friend, did he win anything?'

'No. I'd cracked his favourite pole,' she said bluntly. Let him make a joke out of that and she would throw her coffee in his face. She should have known better.

How could a villain like Luc Di Maggi appreciate the work and effort that went into just getting to the Olympics? Whatever Di Maggi wanted he got by any crooked means he could.

'It could only happen to you, Parisa.' He shook his dark head. 'You cracked h...' Jumping to his feet, rubbing a large tanned hand over his mouth, he muttered, 'I need to shave,' and shot out of the room...

The man was obviously not quite sane, Parisa thought, as the sound of his laughter reached her from the bathroom. The temptation to get up and walk out was almost overwhelming. She actually got to her feet and walked into the hall. Only the thought of Moya's cries of the night before echoing in her head stayed her footsteps. No. She had promised; she had to go through with it. But had she?

The sitting-room door was invitingly open. She listened. The sound of running water told her Luc was still busy. Quietly she entered the room, crossed to the sideboard, and slowly opened the drawer. Her blue eyes gleamed triumphantly at the sight of the incriminating package. Carefully she picked it up and, spinning on her heel, ran swiftly back out of the room into the hall, and was soon at the front door, a smug smile of satisfaction tilting her full lips as her hand turned the brass doorknob. It had been so easy. She couldn't believe her luck... Damn! she cursed under her breath, twisting the knob the opposite way.

'I think you will find you need this...'

Slowly she turned. Luc was leaning against the wall about two feet away, his arm outstretched, a key dangling from his long fingers. She looked at him, and in that moment the full force of her actions over the past dozen hours hit her like a ton of bricks. A shiver of fear snaked down her spine. Too late she remembered that this man was a criminal, and would stop at nothing to get what he wanted. With wary eyes she studied his still body, the firm, well-muscled contours of it now dressed casually in hip-hugging jeans and a black crew-neck cashmere sweater. She was forcibly made aware of the threatening, predatory character of the man.

While she had been disarmed by his friendly chatter over coffee he had been one step ahead all the time. He must have locked the door and removed the key as soon as she had arrived and now he was poised like some jungle panther ready to spring.

Parisa flushed hotly as Luc's gaze, black and hard as jet, swept over her, his eyes resting on the package she held in her hand. 'So, still trying to steal and run,' he drawled, slipping the key in his trouser pocket as he moved towards her. 'The car in the back lane again, I presume.'

'Presume away,' she snapped, avoiding his eyes. His hand curled around her wrist, and with his other hand he removed the package from her trembling fingers.

'Mine, I believe.' His mouth twisted cynically as he carelessly flung the photos on the hall table, adding, 'Unless you feel like earning them, Parisa, hmm?' and, grasping her chin between his thumb and finger, he tilted her head back so that she was forced to look at him.

She was angry and frightened, but she fought not to show it, and would have succeeded except suddenly she was aware of the closeness of his large body, the clean scent of him fresh from the shower. She tried to pull away, but his hand tightened on her jaw and a fierce sexual tension shimmered in the air.

She saw red at the darkening sensual glitter that flickered in his hard gaze. 'You're disgusting. Moya told me your terms—cash or kind—but you don't scare me. You, you sex maniac, you,' she spluttered, more afraid than furious.

He raised one dark brow. '"In kind", is that right?' He watched her for a moment in silence, then, letting go of her wrist, but still holding her chin, he ran one long finger around the outline of her lips. 'Yes, it might almost be worth it. Though most women wait until they are asked,' he commented sardonically.

She flushed. 'Why, you conceited——'

'*Basta*, Parisa, I will hear no more insults from you. Either you come to Italy with me on Monday as we agreed last night, or I send the photographs to the newspapers. The decision is yours, but I can assure you you have nothing to fear on the sexual front from me. I prefer my women slightly smaller, slightly fuller, and a lot more willing.' His hand fell from her chin and he stepped back, his handsome face devoid of all expression. 'I am hungry. You can tell me your final decision over breakfast. Wait!' And, turning his back on her, he picked up the photographs and walked into the bedroom.

Parisa watched him go with an angry frown. She did not know whether to be insulted or pleased that he did not fancy her. He had had no such qualms about her voluptuous friend Moya. But at least she supposed it was reassuring.

'Ready to leave now?' he demanded curtly.

He was still angry, she recognised, considering him warily as he pulled on a coat. 'I thought you wanted breakfast,' she could not help saying.

'I do, and that is where we are going.'

'Can't you cook?'

'If that is an offer, thanks.' He smiled, and her heart jumped at the easy charm on his face. She was vividly reminded of the first time he had ever smiled at her so long ago. 'But there's no food in the apartment,' he added ruefully.

Half an hour later, sitting opposite Luc at an elegantly laid table in the dining-room of a top London hotel, she stared in amazement as he tucked into a full English breakfast of bacon, eggs, sausage, mushrooms, tomatoes and toast. She sipped from a small china cup what was her fifth dose of coffee that morning, and thought again of his warm smile. He was an odd man.

One minute he had been furious and the next he had been smiling at her as though they were friends.

'Have you decided?'

Parisa choked on her coffee, and glanced across the table. 'How could you possibly eat all that in the morning?' she asked, trying to change the subject.

'Easy. I'm a big man, in case you hadn't noticed. I have a big appetite...' A lazy smile curved his hard mouth. 'Now answer my question,' he drawled, his gaze resting on her flushed face.

She would go to Italy with him—she had already promised Moya—but, sitting in the hotel dining-room looking at Luc, an attractive, well-fed, relaxed male, she could not help trying to appeal to his better nature just once.

'Luc, I can't believe you need money so badly, or that you would break up Moya's engagement for the hell of it. She is very much in love with Simon; they dropped me off at your place today, on their way to buy the wedding rings. Why not give me the photographs and forget about it? Just this once.' She watched his handsome face, hoping to see some kind of acceptance. Instead his jaw tightened, and she noticed a muscle jerk in his cheek.

'"Just this once"...' he drawled cynically. 'Am I supposed to be flattered that you considered appealing to me?' One dark brow arched enquiringly. 'What about all my other victims? Are they no less deserving of my sympathy?'

'I don't care about the rest, Luc. If you'll just forget about Moya, I promise no one will ever hear a word from me about your business,' she said earnestly.

'I'm relieved to hear it,' he told her, his mouth tightening in a thin line. 'But it is no deal. All I want from you is a "Yes" or "No".'

Parisa looked up sharply, meeting his gaze with angry wide blue eyes. 'Yes, damn you! I will come to Italy with you, for two days. I will pretend to be your fiancée, and on Wednesday I want those photographs.' She stood up. She should have had more sense than to appeal to Luc's better nature. He didn't have one.

'Good. In that case we will follow your friends' example and go shopping for the ring.' Tugging her small hand firmly under his arm, he led her out of the restaurant and to her astonishment stopped at a large black limousine complete with chauffeur, parked outside the hotel.

'Good morning, Mr Di Maggi. Nice to see you again,' the uniformed driver greeted him, opening the rear door.

'Good morning, Johnson.' And as Parisa stood with her mouth hanging open, Luc urged her into the car. She could not understand it: they had taken a taxi to the hotel. 'The jeweller's, please, Johnson,' he commanded and slid the glass partition between driver and passengers closed, before settling back against the soft leather upholstery.

'My God! Who said crime doesn't pay?' Parisa exclaimed involuntarily, her blue eyes huge as saucers in her beautiful face.

Luc shot her a quelling sidelong glance. 'I always hire a limousine when I am in London. The parking is so terrible that there is no point in keeping a car. But before we go any further, I want to get one point straight. For the next few days, you will refrain from calling me a criminal. To my friends and family I am a businessman,' he said curtly.

Some business, she thought, but one look at his face and she wisely kept her opinions to herself. Instead she asked, 'Is it really necessary to buy a ring? I don't really have time. I have to go home. I'll need to tell my...' She almost said housekeeper, but stopped in time. 'I have to pack...' She was gabbling, but in the close confines of the car Luc's nearness was vaguely intimidating. No, not vaguely, but seriously intimidating, she thought, shooting him a nervous glance. Her leg burned through the soft hide of her skirt where his muscular thigh pressed against her. Was he doing it deliberately? No, of course not, she told herself, looking out of the window; the car was turning a corner.

'Yes, a ring is essential, and don't worry—I'll take you home. Then I'll know where to collect you on Monday morning,' he said smoothly, adding, 'Unfortunately I have business to attend to tonight and tomorrow or we could have spent the time practising acting as lovers!' His dark eyes flashed a mocking message, but Parisa did not respond. A vivid image of Luc and Margot Mey in each other's arms flashed in her mind. A cynical smile twisted her full lips. She knew just what his business was this weekend.

If she needed any confirmation she got it at the jeweller's. The assistant greeted Luc with a broad smile. 'Back so soon, Mr Di Maggi? Was there something wrong with the bracelet you bought yesterday?'

Parisa almost laughed out loud. She was forced to go to Italy for the sake of her friend, but she obviously had nothing at all to fear from Luc Di Maggi, as, with a suave smile, he responded to the assistant.

'No, the bracelet is perfect and I'm sure the lady will appreciate it. But it is rings I wish to see today.'

The assistant gave Parisa an apologetic smile, and some imp of mischief, or maybe it was pure feminine pride, made her declare, 'I want to see your biggest, flashiest costume rings—something that looks like the Koh-i-noor.' She would act like one of his tarty mistresses, and see how he liked it.

The man looked at Luc, and after a brief exchange in Italian and a nod of Luc's dark head the man disappeared and returned a few minutes later with a tray of rings.

Parisa picked the biggest one. It was a huge slightly blue stone and couldn't possibly be real, but she slipped it on her finger and it fitted perfectly.

'I love this one, Luc, darling,' she drawled, turning a patently false smile on her companion.

'Are you sure, Parisa? There is a wide selection.' Luc's dark eyes, glittering with suppressed anger, captured hers.

'Positive, dearest,' she simpered, thoroughly enjoying herself. But ten minutes later, back in the car with a darkly brooding stranger at her side, she wished she had not tried to bait him.

The car drew to a halt. The chauffeur got out and opened Parisa's door. She looked across at Luc.

'Here, Monday, ten a.m., and don't forget your ring.'

'Certainly,' she murmured.

CHAPTER THREE

PARISA let herself into the apartment with the key Moya had given her. It was a ground-floor flat in a block of four converted from an old terrace house in Kensington. She went straight to the telephone and ordered a taxi to the railway station. It had been a stroke of genius, allowing Luc Di Maggi to think she shared Moya's apartment in London. This way, when their brief sojourn on the Continent was over there was no danger of him ever finding her again. Moya was leaving next weekend for her father's house in Norfolk and after the wedding would take up residence in Sussex. If Parisa could just get through the next few days and retrieve the photographs, everything would be fine. It took a matter of minutes to pack her clothes. She wrote a note to Moya, assuring her everything was under control and telling her to expect her back on Sunday evening. Then once again she left the apartment.

She breathed a deep sigh of satisfaction some three hours later as the local taxi stopped outside the massive entrance door to Hardcourt Manor. She paid the driver and swiftly ran up the stone steps and into the house. She flung her bag on the battered table in the large oak-panelled hall and shouted, 'Didi, darling, I'm back.'

A small, stooped grey-haired lady appeared from the back of the house. 'You don't need to shout. I am not deaf, my girl.'

Parisa laughed out loud and put her arms around the frail lady, giving her a brief hug. 'I'm sorry, Didi, but I'm so glad to be home.'

'You have only been gone one night. It's not right, a lovely young woman burying herself in the country. You

40

should have stayed in London, enjoyed yourself. Joe and I are quite all right on our own.'

'I know, Didi, and spare me the lecture. I have a dinner date with David tonight.' Parisa grinned. 'And I'm going back to London tomorrow for a few more days' holiday. Your wish is answered. Satisfied?'

'Certainly, but what's this?' and, grasping Parisa's hand, she eyed the huge ring.

Parisa flushed and pulled her hand free. 'Nothing— I bought it for fun,' she mumbled.

'Hmmph. Some fun. You should get a man to buy you jewels, a lovely girl like you. I can't see David Brown exactly sweeping you off your feet.'

'Please, Didi, don't start.' David was not her house-keeper's idea of a matrimonial prospect. She considered the man far too tame. 'Be a dear, I'm gasping for tea.' Parisa, blue eyes shining, watched the little old lady disappear through the door at the back of the stairs. She knew what Didi meant, though. David was thirty years old. He lived with his mother in Battle, and Parisa had been dating him for about a year. They shared a meal together or visited the theatre in Brighton about once a month, and they both looked after the scout troop. He was tall and fair—quite handsome in fact. Parisa liked him because he was a good conversationalist and a fine friend. He was not a demonstrative man, and the good-night kisses they shared were warm and comforting, but not in the least threatening. Nothing like Luc Di Maggi's passionate embrace... The errant thought flashed in her mind, but she quickly squashed it.

Parisa ran lightly up the stairs. God knew what Didi would say if she knew the truth! Parisa thought wryly. She was going off to Italy with a man, and a villain to boot... But hopefully Didi would never find out, and, pulling the ring from her finger, she dropped it in her bag.

Didi was the housekeeper, but more like a mother to Parisa. When her own parents died, her guardians were

the family solicitor and her grandmother. After the death
of her grandmother, only months after that of her
parents, the solicitor had quite happily left the young
girl in Didi's care. Parisa loved her dearly and would
never do anything to hurt her.

Parisa's smooth brow creased in a worried frown as
she reached the top of the staircase and automatically
avoided the tattered part of the stair carpet. If her solicitor did not come up with a solution soon, the house
was liable to fall down around her head, she mused, and
what would become of Didi and Joe? Parisa loved being
a sports teacher, but the salary was nowhere near enough
to support the crumbling manor and its inhabitants. Mr
Jarvis was a kindly old man, but she sometimes wished
he hadn't waited until she was twenty-one and had finished college before explaining fully the desperate state
of her finances. It was a huge responsibility, being the
last living Hardcourt and custodian of the old manor
house and the old couple...

Later, after sharing an evening meal with David at a
small hotel in Hailsham, and with the lingering taste of
his goodnight kiss on her lips, Parisa, feeling warm and
reasonably content, stripped off her clothes in her
bedroom. Pulling a wool nightshirt over her head, she
scrambled quickly into the huge four-poster bed, and
snuggled down under the layers of blankets. Experience
had taught her that warmth was something to be con-
served in a house where the ancient central heating went
out with the fire and the blustery February winds whistled
through every nook and cranny of the old building.

She closed her eyes, and for a moment an image of a
dark-haired black-eyed man lingered in her mind. She
touched a finger to her lips, but it wasn't David's kiss
she recalled, but the fierce passion of Luc Di Maggi's
lips. She shivered, but not with the cold. She wondered
what Luc was doing now, and remembered Margot Mey.
She knew exactly what Luc was doing, and told herself

she was glad. It would make the next few days much easier for her...

She stood on the pavement: a tall, slender girl, her long blonde hair swept back and tied with a bright blue silk scarf at her nape, to fall down past her shoulder-blades in a swathe of silver gilt. The colour of the scarf matched the brilliant blue of her eyes and the crew-necked sweater that peeped from the lapels of a soft camel overcoat. The coat was wrapped firmly around her narrow waist and held with a matching belt. On her feet she wore cream leather flat-heeled boots, and over her shoulder was slung a matching handbag. On the ground at her side stood a battered but obviously good leather suitcase.

Parisa stamped her feet against the cold and also to ease the tension. She had suggested last night that Moya might like to make one last appeal to Luc Di Maggi, but her friend had flatly refused even to see the man, and after her friend's crying bout Parisa had given up pursuing the idea. Which was why she was waiting on the pavement instead of in the apartment: Moya was frantic at the thought of Luc even reaching the door.

She glanced at the slender gold watch circling her wrist. Five past ten—he was late. Her eye caught the flashing ring on her finger; it was too large for her one decent pair of kid gloves to fit over, and her hand was freezing. Served her right, she thought, smiling wryly.

'Admiring your ring, Parisa?' The deep, melodious voice made her jump with fear. She swirled around, her eyes widening as she looked up into the handsome face of Luc Di Maggi. He caught her arm, as she would have stepped back into the road. 'Careful, Parisa,' he said curtly, pulling her back against him so that she landed flat against his broad chest. 'I don't want to see you run over; at least, not before you fulfil your part of our bargain.'

'You're late,' she said angrily, staring up at him in frustration. Why did she always seem to end up in his arms? She hadn't even noticed the car pull up a few yards away...

A brief smile curled his lips. 'Did you miss me?' He raised one eyebrow mockingly and, turning her in his arms, he caught her bare hand in his, and with fluid ease picked up her suitcase with his free hand.

She had finally run out of time and choices. With her small, cold hand quickly warming beneath the pressure of his long fingers, she meekly followed him. She cast a surreptitious glance at the man by her side. He was looking straight ahead. His handsome profile looked as though it were hewn out of granite. A dark navy overcoat fitted snugly across his wide shoulders, the collar turned up at his neck against the chill of the morning, the heavy wool falling in a smooth flow to mid calf. His black hair, his dark eyes, the tanned complexion, his smooth, arrogant stride, even his clothes all cried macho Italian male. Uneasily she recalled the rumours at school about Tina, the girl with the Mafia connections!

It was just stupid schoolgirl gossip, she told herself reassuringly, but, as she stood by the long black limousine while the chauffeur packed her case in the boot she wasn't so sure.

'Get in the car,' Luc said curtly, and she did.

An hour later, as she walked up the steps to the waiting Lear Jet, her suspicions had grown to gigantic proportions. Luc had whisked her through Gatwick airport, the Customs, and out to the plane without speaking a word, and as she entered the cabin of the aircraft and looked around her she felt a sinking feeling in the pit of her stomach.

A dark-suited man asked, 'May I take your coat?' Too stunned to protest, she untied the belt and allowed the man to slip it from her shoulders. 'Take-off is in five minutes. Please be seated.'

He led her, unprotesting, across deep, plush green carpet, past two soft leather sofas and matching armchairs and a gilt-edged coffee table, to where a row of aircraft seats were placed at the rear of the plane. She sat down, her blue eyes wide with amazement. A private plane, no less.

She looked up to find Luc towering over her. With a shrug of his broad shoulders he handed his overcoat to the waiting steward and settled his huge frame in the seat next to her.

'Who does this plane belong to?' she demanded.

'The company, of course. Now fasten your seatbelt, Parisa.' And he deftly flicked the catch on his own.

She turned her head away from his dark presence and looked out of the window. The company! Oh, my God! she thought helplessly, was that another name for the Mafia? What did she know? No casino manager, however well paid, swanned around in chauffeur-driven limousines, or used private airplanes. Luc might possibly have saved and bought the casino, but he was obviously no small-time crook. Her own bet was he was probably a member of or had connections to an organised crime syndicate! After all, what did she really know about Luc Di Maggi? She had met the man three times in ten years. What had she got herself into? she wondered fearfully.

She looked down, fumbling with her seatbelt, and a strong arm stretched in front of her, the sleeve of his sweater brushing lightly across her breasts. Instantly tense, she turned back to the window as long fingers clipped the catch firmly closed. Her fear turned to terror, and her mind went blank. She held her breath as the ground rushed away from them. Her heart racing, her hands clutched at the arm rests, knuckles white with the force of her grip.

A large, warm hand covered hers, and she clung, her nails digging into the hard flesh. She didn't care what she was revealing; she hated flying.

'The impulsive Parisa, scared of flying,' a mocking voice drawled in her ear.

'I am not,' she lied. 'I just don't like the take-off and landing, and I'm not impulsive,' she said through clenched teeth.

Luc, his dark head turned towards her, his eyes lit with unholy amusement, caught her tense gaze. 'No? You're on this plane, engaged to a man you hardly know, and no idea of your destination . . .' His lips curled back over perfect white teeth in a wicked grin, and she wanted to thump him. 'I would say that is pretty impulsive by anyone's standards.'

He was right, and she hated him for it. The one thing she prided herself on was being a calm, rational adult woman, but her own innate honesty forced her to admit that for the past few days she had acted recklessly, to say the least. But with Moya's happiness at stake, she had had no choice! Slowly she eased her hand from his and, looking down, unfastened her seatbelt, avoiding his laughing black eyes.

'No comeback, Parisa?' he mocked and, unclipping his seatbelt, he pushed his long legs out in front of him.

Blue eyes flashing angrily, she turned to him. 'Yes . . . No . . .' she stammered, her stomach lurching at the sight of him. He was stretching his long arms above his head like a great jungle cat, his black trousers pulled taut across his hard thighs. The soft cream and black crew-necked sweater, which moulded his muscular chest, rose up, revealing a bare tanned midriff with a teasing line of black hair. She could not seem to tear her eyes away from the patch of tanned skin. She felt the colour flood her face as the steward spoke.

'Would the lady like coffee, breakfast?'

She looked up, her face burning. 'Just coffee, please.'

Luc stood up. 'The lot for me, please, Max.' And, stooping slightly, he held out one strong hand to Parisa. 'Come along, we may as well make ourselves comfortable. We have a lot of ground to cover in the next few hours, both literally and figuratively speaking.'

She ignored his hand and rose to her feet. His sensuous mouth twisted in a cynical smile at her obvious action, but he made no comment, simply walked across to an armchair placed beside the coffee-table, and lowered his huge frame into it.

'What do you mean, figuratively?' she asked warily, moving to a sofa at the opposite side of the table. His dark eyes followed her every step of the way. Studying her, from the top of her pale blonde head, down over the proud tilt of her breasts against the smooth wool of her sweater to her narrow waist, bound by a tan leather belt, and on over her slim hips in the short straight blue and beige tweed skirt, to the soft curve of her calves, and her short boots. 'You have great legs,' he said, ignoring her question.

'My legs are no concern of yours,' she said flatly, sitting down on the sofa, and self-consciously trying to pull her skirt over her knees. 'We have a bargain, you and I: two days with your mother, and I get Moya's photographs.' She was desperate to redefine the limit of their relationship, to quell her mounting fear.

The steward arrived and placed a loaded tray on the table. In seconds a steaming cup of coffee was in front of Parisa. As for Luc, a plate of ham and eggs was placed in front of him.

He looked down at the plate as she watched, and then lifted his head, his black eyes catching hers. 'You're right, of course, Parisa. By figuratively I meant we have to appear to know each other intimately.'

She stiffened, her hand stopping on the cup, her imagination going into overdrive: a vivid image of Luc as he had been on Saturday morning, part naked, and herself enfolded in his strong arms. To know him intimately! She shivered at the thought and felt the colour rise in her cheeks.

'No, not in the biblical sense,' he drawled mockingly, easily reading her mind. 'But my mother is an intelligent and very astute woman. She will expect me to know your

family, your past history, that sort of thing, Lady Parisa.'
And, picking up a knife and fork, he added, 'While I
eat, perhaps you will oblige, hmm?' Turning his attention to the food in front of him, he proceeded to eat.

She took a deep breath, reminding herself wryly that
she was a mature woman, not a stupid teenager in-
dulging in erotic thoughts, and Luc's request was
reasonable, she supposed. 'Well, for a start I am not a
Lady.'

A burst of laughter greeted her remark. 'Thank God
you said that, and not some unsuspecting male. No doubt
you would slap his face.' Luc grinned.

'I didn't mean it like that,' she said, flustered by his
open grin. 'My father was Lord of Hardcourt Manor—
the title went with the estate. When my parents died,
and then my grandmother, six months later, leaving me
the last of the line, I suppose some people automatically
assumed I should be addressed as Lady Hardcourt-
Belmont. But it doesn't really apply any more.'

'Because you live in London now,' Luc said, adding,
'How old were you when your parents died?'

'Fourteen.'

'Before I met you.'

'Yes. Anyway, I left school.'

'How did they die?'

'My father was a budding racing driver when he met
Mother. Later he tried powerboat racing, then he
changed to hot-air ballooning, and they went missing
over the Atlantic in a balloon. Satisfied?' She didn't like
talking about their death. She had been completely devastated. They had been such a laughing, happy family,
and she had felt so lost. Then her grandmother had spent
the last few months of her life impressing upon Parisa
that she was the sole heir, and stressing the responsi-
bilities that went with it, pointing out the dangers of
impulsive behaviour—and then her grandmother had
died as well. Parisa had cried herself to sleep for months.
Didi and Joe had done their best but it wasn't quite the

same as one's own family. Over the years she had found
the loss easier to manage. But it still hurt, and the lone-
liness lingered.

'You take after him.'

'No, I do not.' She had loved her parents dearly, but
she had spent most of her adult life determined to quell
any spark of recklessness in her own nature.

'All right, don't get excited. Who took care of you
when you lost your parents and grandmother?'

She looked across the table and was surprised to see
a fleeting glimpse of some emotion in his black eyes.

'The family solicitor. Anyway, I finished school, went
to university, and I now teach sport at an independent
school, south of London, in Sussex.' She hurried to finish
her life history, telling the truth, but not all. 'Now, what
about you?' she asked. 'I know you're Italian and have
a mother and cousin Tina. You successfully blackmail
people, enough to buy a casino, and probably have quite
a few dubious connections if this plane is anything to
go by. Do I need to know any more?' she asked snidely.

For a second she thought she had gone too far. His
tanned face flushed dark with some inner rage; his black
eyes narrowed on her face, hard as ice. She watched as
his fingers clenched on the knife in his hand. But by a
terrific effort of will he brought his rage under control
and leant back in the chair.

'No. I think you have me covered very well, Parisa.
Now, if you will excuse me, I have some business to
attend to.' And, picking up a briefcase from the side of
the chair, he shoved the plate and cups along the table,
banged the case down, and opened it. Withdrawing some
papers, he began to read, completely ignoring Parisa.

She was pleased, she told herself, and, laying her head
back against the sofa, she closed her eyes, pretending to
sleep. For three days she had been living in a state of
nervous tension, and finally nature had caught up with
her. She felt her eyelids droop, and her last conscious
thought was that he had not denied her taunt about his

other crooked activities... The trip to Italy was forced upon her: there was no way she could have lived with herself if she had allowed Luc to destroy Moya's life; but she had to be on her guard at all times...

Parisa stirred, her lips parting on a sigh. She was curled up comfortably, her head resting against soft fabric, one hand burrowed between hard heat and soft warmth. She rubbed her face against the welcoming wool, trying to ignore the low sounds bringing her back to consciousness. With a wide yawn she opened her eyes. For a moment she was disorientated.

'We have almost reached our destination, Parisa.'

Oh, God! Her head was nestled against a very masculine shoulder, but worse—much worse—somehow one hand had slipped very intimately under his sweater to the tanned midriff she had admired earlier. She jerked upright, her face flushing crimson. She looked sideways at Luc. He was watching her, his dark eyes amused, and with a trace of something more she refused to acknowledge.

'My...my hand. I'm sorry... You should have woken me...' She stuttered to an embarrassed halt.

'Don't be—I am not. Frustrating, but very pleasant,' he opined smoothly. 'Unfortunately we are about to land in five minutes.'

Parisa jumped off the sofa and almost ran to the aircraft seat, and buckled herself in without daring to look at him. She should have known better than to try to apologise. The man was a sex maniac, with his Margot, and trying it on with Moya and heaven knew how many more.

Gritting her teeth as he sat down beside her once again, she closed her eyes and made herself keep her hands tightly clasped in her lap. Refusing to give in to the terror the ground rushing up to meet them induced in her, she opened her eyes.

'Oh, my God! The sea!' she exclaimed, and all her good intentions flew out of the window as she grabbed Luc's arm with both hands.

'Genoa Airport—the approach is over the sea,' Luc said calmly. 'Nothing to worry about.'

She turned frightened eyes up to his and, before she could speak, his dark head bent and his mouth covered hers, hot and hard against her softly parted lips. She stared up at him through a hazy blackness. Her breath stopped. His tongue touched hers, teased the roof of her mouth, and she closed her eyes against the blazing light she saw in his. Her pulse rocketed as the most shocking hot, pleasurable sensation rushed through her. His groan of pleasure made her realise just what she was doing, and she began to struggle, but suddenly she was free.

Luc leant back in his seat, and calmly unfastened his seatbelt.

'You had no right to do that...' Parisa spluttered, amazed at his cool control when she felt as though she had been run over by a ten-ton truck. 'Our bargain is strictly business.'

'So it is, Parisa, but you've got to admit it worked: you never noticed the landing.'

She glanced out of the window. He was right, damn him! Silently fuming at his arrogance, she swiftly unfastened the seatbelt, picked her handbag off the floor and, making sure he moved first, she slowly stood up. The steward held out her coat, and she slipped it on, tying the belt around her small waist with a vicious tug. She was still shaking from the force of his kiss, and hating herself for it. That is the last time he will catch me like that, she swore, as she meekly followed Luc's broad back down the steps of the airplane. Think of David, she told herself.

The Customs officer appeared to know Luc, as the two men conversed in rapid Italian. Parisa, standing stiffly with her passport held in front of her, hadn't a clue what was said, but recognised 'fidanzata' The officer turned to her, a brilliant smile on his olive-skinned face, and by the voluble speech he made she guessed he was congratulating her. She gave him a weak smile in return, and muttered one of the few Italian words she knew. '*Grazie.*'

Luc smiled down at her from his great height. 'You speak my language, *cara*,' he mocked and, taking her arm, ushered her out of the terminal to a lethal red car.

She eyed the long, low vehicle warily. She knew very little about motors, but even she recognised the formidable lines of a Ferrari, and she knew they did not come cheap. More and more, she was convinced he must be a big-time crook. The few thousand Luc had demanded from Moya could only be a drop in the ocean to a man who flew in private planes and owned such a car. So why the blackmail? She glanced uneasily at her companion as he bowed courteously to open the passenger door and stood, back straightening to his full height. Maybe he had never wanted the money, only Moya in his bed. As a gangster, he would have no moral compunction about how he got any woman he fancied.

'Get in,' he commanded. Catching her wary eyes on him, he added, 'You will be perfectly safe. I am an excellent driver.'

She did not doubt it for a minute. This dark, arrogant, ruthless man had the uncanny ability to do anything he wanted to do. She was sure of it. Parisa shivered and slid into the car. She was completely out of her depth and she knew it. Quickly fastening the safety-belt, she flicked a wary glance at Luc as he climbed into the driving seat.

'Does your mother live in Genoa?' she asked politely, making up her mind to get through the next forty-eight hours with the least possible aggravation. It was none of her business what he did, or who with, she told herself. The less she knew about him, the better...

'Sometimes, but I have a villa along the coast at Portofino. The party is to be held there.'

'How nice. I have heard of the place—didn't Rex Harrison live there at one time?' she asked, making social conversation.

'I believe so.' Luc cast her a brief sidelong glance. 'But you have no need to pretend with me, Parisa. Save your act for when you meet my mother.'

Right, you swine, I will, she thought mutinously. So much for being polite... For the rest of the journey she stared out of the window, and eventually, as they left the city built on the hillside, she became fascinated by the rugged coastline, the colour-washed stone cottages, and the deep blue of the Mediterranean.

From the warmth of the car she could almost believe it was a summer's day. The sun was shining, the sky was a clear blue, and only the bright green shoots, the fresh buds and the soft unfurling of an occasional leaf on the passing trees told her it was barely spring. The car swung to the left between two massive stone pillars topped off with the sculpted head of lions, and they were travelling up a dark avenue of tall deep green pine trees.

Suddenly the car was in brilliant sun again, and Parisa could not help her gasp of amazement. On what looked like the top of a cliff was the most fantastic villa she had ever seen.

Luc stopped the car and turned towards her. 'You like my home?' he asked, a devilish twinkle lighting his dark eyes, and the smile on his handsome face almost boyish.

It was a joke, a fantasy. Parisa could not stop her lips curving in a smile. 'I don't believe it,' she said in awe. Before them was a huge circular pink-washed building with white stone trimming around long, arched windows. Halfway up the wall, at the first floor, a delicate, ornate white ironwork balcony circled the building, beneath another set of arched windows. It was a bit like a light-house, but squatter, with a massive arched entrance door. But it was the roof that truly caught the eye: almost white tiles rising to the centre, and another circular room with a domed copper top.

'It looks like a giant birthday cake,' she chuckled. 'I can't believe anyone would build a house like that.'

'Neither could I when I first saw it,' Luc said wryly. 'Some rock star in the sixties designed and built it. The roof-top room is an observatory. Apparently he enjoyed watching the stars as well as being one. I bought it because it is on a prime piece of land, and with the intention of pulling it down and rebuilding, but somehow I fell in love with the place; eccentric and not at all like me...but...' He gave a very Latin shrug and a rather wry smile.

Parisa was still grinning as Luc helped her out of the car, and, with a hand cupping her elbow, led her up the marble steps to the great door. Before they reached the top step, the door was flung open, and a magnificent white-haired lady dressed all in black flung her arms wide and Luc, releasing Parisa, stepped into them.

Parisa stared. His little old mother in bad health was almost six feet tall and huge with it. It was obvious who Luc took after, she thought, watching the embracing couple.

'Parisa, darling, allow me to introduce you. My mother.'

Her mouth fell open at the darling, and quickly she closed it again. Taking the last step, she held out her small hand to the old lady.

'How do you do?' she said softly. Her hand was tugged, and before she knew what was happening she was folded against a more than ample bosom in a great bear-hug.

'No formality. You—you, my child, will be my daughter.' And Parisa was soundly kissed on both cheeks before being set free. She looked into the dark, sparkling eyes of the older woman and was touched to see them moist. 'Come. Come inside...'

Parisa did not know how it happened, but within minutes she was divested of her coat and seated in the curve of Luc's arm on a comfortable sofa in a beautiful room, one wall of which was curved with elegant windows. Rich blue velvet drapes, braided and tasselled, shaded the bright sunlight from the soft cream furnishings. The obviously excellent paintings and *objets d'art* scattered around all screamed good taste and great wealth.

'We must have champagne...a toast... Yes...'

Parisa shook her head in an effort to clear her thoughts, and tensed as Luc spoke softly, his breath warm against her ear.

'Remember why you are here. Upset my mother, and I will make you pay.'

Startled by the threat in his whispered words, she glared suspiciously at him. For a moment she had forgotten he was her enemy and had found comfort in his protective arm about her shoulders.

'What do you mean?' she asked, puzzled by his anger.

'I will not allow you to dismiss my mother with a toss of your elegant head. You will accept the champagne and smile,' he hissed with sibilant softness, so only she could hear.

He was wrong about her action. It had not been a refusal, but now was not the time to argue, and, turning, she smiled at the other woman, and in a calm voice said, 'Yes, I would love some champagne.'

A smart dark-suited young man appeared, carrying an ice-bucket with the plump gold-topped bottle nestling inside, and a tray bearing fine crystal glasses, which he placed on the table by the old lady. The young man picked up the bottle and with swift expertise opened it. The cork flew across the room and bounced off Parisa's thigh.

'That is good luck, Parisa,' Signora Di Maggi cried delightedly, but Parisa wasn't so sure, as she almost jumped out of her skin in surprise. But when Luc held out a brimming glass she took it, her fingers brushed his, and she flinched at the contact. She told herself it was with loathing.

'To Parisa, my betrothed. May we have a long and happy union,' Luc said, raising his glass, but the dark knowing look in his brilliant eyes told her he had noticed her reaction and was amused by it.

Bravely she raised her own glass and sipped the sparkling liquid. She accepted his mother's effusive congratulations in a mixture of Italian and English with as much grace as she could muster, blushing furiously when the old lady exclaimed over the beauty of the engagement ring, and conscious all the time of Luc's dark eyes watching her, waiting to pounce on her least mistake.

She heaved an inward sigh of relief when his mother suggested, 'You must be tired. So long you travel. Luc will show you your room. We will talk later tonight, before the mob arrive, yes?'

Out in the huge circular hall Parisa turned baleful eyes on Luc. 'Your poor, weak little mother,' she sneered. 'What a liar you are—the woman is built like an amazon and looks as fit as a fiddle.' She used anger to hide her fear: the old lady had quite openly mentioned the mob. Was that not another name for the Mafia?

'Shut up and follow me,' and, striding to a wide marble staircase, he ascended the stairs.

He was doing it again. Follow me! Parisa fumed, but had no real alternative but to do what he said. How in God's name she had got herself in this mess? She couldn't believe it. Perhaps she did have some of the wild Hardcourt genes after all, and the thought terrified her. She had spent years convincing herself she was safe from that particular hereditary fault, but now she was not so sure.

'This is your room. I trust you will be comfortable here. If you need anything, there is a bell-rope beside the bed. I am in the room next door.'

Her head shot back and she looked up at him, not at all happy at the thought of only a single wall separating her from Luc.

'I'm sure it will be fine, thank you,' she replied formally, successfully masking her apprehension. She glanced around the room. It was beautifully decorated in soft white and pale rose, entirely feminine, but exquisite. A queen-sized bed, the coverlet delicately embroidered white lace with a pink undercover. A small satin settee was at one side of a real fireplace, the surround of which was in a white and pink veined marble with a brass grate and antique fender. The dressing-table was built into one of the straight walls, along with mirrored wardrobes and a door.

A large hand curved around her shoulder and she tensed defensively; she had not realised Luc was so close. 'The bathroom is that door.' Luc gestured with his free hand.

'Thank you,' she said, wishing he would leave.

'So polite, when not five minutes ago you were calling me a liar. There is a penalty for that kind of talk, Parisa,' he informed her silkily.

She should have known he would not let her comment about his mother go unanswered.

'I warned you before, but obviously you need a few more lessons in how to behave as my fiancée.'

His strong arms locked around her. She tried to push him away. 'Really, Luc, aren't you being rather childish?' she admonished. But the hard intent in his black eyes barely wavered at her ineffectual attempt to break free. 'Let go...' was as far as she got.

His dark head lowered. She turned her head to the side, determined to avoid him. But when his teeth bit lightly on her exposed neck, she shuddered. If anything it was worse than a kiss. His lips trailed up and over her jaw, while all the time his arms kept her pressed tightly against his hard body. She could feel the steady pounding of his heart, the deep, appreciative growl, as his mouth finally found hers, and within seconds she was lost in the expertise of his kiss.

It didn't matter what or who he was, she thought wildly. He just had to touch her and a million nerve-ends caught fire. What was happening to her? David never had this startling effect on her, and she liked him. Whereas Luc, a man she despised, with one kiss could turn her bones to jelly. A soft moan escaped her as Luc's lips left hers. Was it regret?

'Interesting, Parisa, wouldn't you say?' he asked throatily. 'An unexpected bonus, my little cat burglar.' She stared, her blue eyes wide and wary. He tipped back her head so he could look down into her flushed face. 'You want me.'

'No...' she husked, fighting for control. She could feel the heavy pressure of his muscular thighs against her long legs, and, more, the hard pulse of his arousal. He might have declared she was not his type, but his body obviously wasn't aware of the fact, she thought, swallowing hard and trying to wriggle away, but to her horror it appeared to arouse him more.

'Hmm. Nice, Parisa, very nice.' He moved his thighs against her.

'No, no, you're mad!' she cried, and with an almighty shove at his chest she tried again to break free.

'Stop fighting, *cara*. You know you want it as much as I do,' he growled, his arm around her waist, lifting her so her feet left the ground and she was helpless in his hold.

His lips nuzzled at her neck and she felt the blood rush through her veins. Her slender hands wrapped around his neck and when she felt his large hand cover her breast through the fine wool of her sweater, her nipple tightened in a sudden aching want. Dear heaven! What was happening to her? She had never felt this way before, but, some imp inside reminded her, she had once—as a young girl, and with the same man.

'We are two consenting adults, Parisa. Don't fight it.' He whispered the words against her mouth before once again his mouth covered hers, his tongue pressed and gained entry, and hot warmth flooded from her mouth to her breast to her loins in a single arrow of delight.

It was only when she felt the softness of the bed at her back that she finally realised what she was inviting and with whom. She panicked, and, striking out wildly, she shot across the bed and off the other side, to stand trembling a couple of feet away.

'You—you animal! Don't touch me!' she cried. Luc sprawled on his back on the bed, his dark eyes searching her flushed face intently. He looked so out of place: huge and dark in his black trousers and cream and black sweater on the white, feminine bed, but the look in his eyes was definitely *come to bed*, Parisa thought, her heart pounding. 'You said I wasn't your type—you promised,' she bit out, stunned by her own response.

'So I've changed my mind, and why not? You enjoy it; as I remember you always did. Before you were too young, but now,' he drawled throatily, 'there is nothing to stop us, hmm?'

She stared at him in amazement. He wasn't angry or joking—he meant it! It was natural for him to have sex with any woman he fancied without a qualm.

'Come back here, Parisa.' He stretched out a large tanned hand coaxingly. 'I promise I will make it good for you.' And he had the gall to smile, a slow twist of his shockingly sensuous lips.

Parisa saw red, and a few other colours besides. The arrogance—the bloody conceit—of the man was unbelievable.

'I wouldn't go to bed with you for all the tea in China,' she fumed. 'You're a blackmailer, a crook, and probably a member of the Mafia. What with your company airplane, your Ferrari, this place——'

To her amazement Luc burst out laughing. 'The Mafia,' he howled, rolling around on the bed. 'Parisa, you are a delight...' he spluttered.

Parisa did not think it the least funny. 'Even your own mother mentioned "the mob". Do you think I'm altogether stupid?'

She had no idea how beautiful she looked. The silk scarf had fallen from her hair, so the platinum mass tumbled around her shoulders in disarray as she stood quivering with anger and the residue of passion, her full breasts taut against the wool of her sweater, her lips swollen from Luc's kisses, and her blue eyes glittering like sapphires in their panic and rage.

Luc's laughter stopped. His dark eyes narrowed, a dull flush swept up his handsome face, and he seemed to catch his breath. Then, very slowly, he sat up, his intent gaze sweeping over the trembling Parisa from head to toe, as though he had never seen her before. He ran his hands through his thick hair, brushing it off his brow, and once more glanced at Parisa.

'What if I said I was not a blackmailer?' he asked softly.

Parisa snorted. 'I wouldn't be here if you weren't.' And she caught a fleeting expression of surprise on Luc's face.

'True,' he admitted, and, rising from the bed, he walked towards the door. He turned with his hand on the handle. 'My mistake, Parisa. I did promise I would not touch you. We dine at eight-thirty. And, by the way, my mother used the word "mob" because her English is not good, no other reason.' And he left, closing the door quietly behind him.

Parisa stared at the door for a long time, not sure what to make of Luc's behaviour. He was a complete enigma to her, one moment making passionate love to her, then a minute later declaring it was a mistake, and in a lightning change of mood he was a polite, sophisticated host. How she wished she had the ability to switch off her emotions so casually.

For some reason she had absolutely no resistance to Luc Di Maggi's particular brand of loving. He was thirty-seven years old, a man of the world, and she could only guess at the kind of world he inhabited. Maybe his mother *had* made a mistake with her English. But Luc had not actually denied being a member of the Mafia. She shivered. This whole episode was light years outside her experience.

She led a quite country life in East Sussex, with an occasional trip to London to the theatre or a show. Apart from being always short of money, she was reasonably content. After the death of her parents and grandmother she had been left pretty much on her own, perhaps because she was considered locally to be a minor aristocrat, and was expected to mix with the hunting and shooting brigade. Although she was a sportswoman, blood sports had never interested her. She found them barbaric, and consequently her social contacts were limited. But the friends she did have, like Moya, and Didi, and a few others, she was intensely loyal to. As for male companionship, she had David. His kisses did not stir her, and she was not serious about him, but he suited her. Nice, uncomplicated David... If only she were with him now.

Luc was not the sort of man anyone would describe as uncomplicated. There was something about him, an aura of strength and power that had nothing to do with his size, but the personality of the man. She should never have come to Italy... It was a bad mistake. She should have talked Moya into calling the police, and let them deal with Luca Di Maggi. For some inexplicable reason, just one glance from Luc's black eyes, one touch of his hand, and she reacted like a giddy teenager. She knew he was a blackmailer. She recalled the tearful, terrified face of her friend. There was no possible doubt that the man was outside the law. So why did she suffer from this intense physical attraction to him? It was crazy. Her common sense told her he was despicable, but her traitorous body blazed at his touch.

She sighed. God, how she wished she were back in England with David. At least with him she was in control. The woman was not born who could control Luca Di Maggi.

CHAPTER FOUR

PARISA told herself to think of the business on hand, to remember Moya. But it wasn't easy. She cupped her breasts to ease the heavy fullness Luc's touch had aroused, and willed the ache in her stomach to subside.

She collapsed on the bed, her head in her hands. Nothing made sense. Moya had called the man a slime ball and opportunist. Yet Luc Di Maggi did not fit that description. A woman would have to be blind or senile not to be aware of the raw masculine appeal of the man. Parisa had kissed a few boys over the years, but none had ever affected her as instantly or as erotically as Luc. Certainly not David.

She felt a twinge of guilt. Poor David. She wasn't serious about him, but she knew he was hoping eventually they would marry, and up until now she had not bothered to disillusion him, being quite happy to have an escort who was safe and reliable. She had not mentioned her trip to Italy on Saturday night, and she realised she had been less than fair to him.

She stood up and walked to the bathroom. Perhaps a cold shower would help clear her brain. If she could get the last three days into focus, maybe she could find the clue to Luc's character, or lack of it . . .

The bathroom knocked every thought out of her head. It was like stepping into a gigantic mirror. She felt herself cringing at the million reflections of herself. A huge circular Jacuzzi followed part way the shape of the outside wall, surrounded by what to Parisa's stunned gaze looked like a platform of jungle plants. There was no way she was climbing in that, she thought, and instead, trying not to look at the walls, stripped off her clothes, and stepped warily into an equally large double shower. She

63

did not linger under the spray: the gold-plated fixtures, and, even worse, the naked couple engraved in the glass shower door, had her face crimson.

Hastily she grabbed a large, fluffy towel from a gold towel rail fixed to the wall by naked gold cherubs, and shot back into the bedroom, wrapping the towel firmly around her. The delicacy of the bedroom seemed at odds with the eroticism of the bathroom. And then she realised she had used the bathroom on the opposite side to the one Luc had indicated. Fast on that thought came the realisation that the bathroom must lead directly to Luc's room, and the knowledge did nothing to calm her over-wrought nerves.

Someone had already unpacked her suitcase, she noted, no longer surprised by anything that happened in this house. She opened the wardrobe door, and found her few clothes neatly hanging in a row. She had only brought two dresses. In fact she only owned two decent formal dresses. She pulled a dark blue velvet dress, the least fancy of the two, from the hanger, and, trying the drawers, she found her underclothes.

Briskly rubbing herself dry, she stepped into a blue lace teddy, with the suspenders attached. She sat down on the bed and carefully pulled silk stockings up her long legs; then, straightening, she slipped the velvet dress over her head. She crossed over to the mirror and smoothed the fabric down over her slim hips.

Not bad, she thought, eyeing her reflection. The dress was a simple fitted sheath with slightly padded shoulders, and long, narrow sleeves ending in a point over her wrists. The skirt was straight and clung to her slender thighs, ending just on her knees.

She sat down at the dressing-table and proceeded to apply the minimum of make-up to her pale face: a light moisturiser, a touch of blue eyeshadow, a sweep of her long lashes with a dark mascara wand, and, to finish, a gentle brush of her cheeks with blusher to add a little colour. She brushed her long hair until it shone like white gold, and deftly swept it up into a chignon on top of her proud head. Lastly she applied a pink lipgloss to her full lips and sprayed her neck and wrist with her favourite perfume: Dior's Dune—a Christmas present from Moya.

Parisa sighed, a feeling of helplessness enveloping her. She had never felt so alone in her life, and she wasn't sure she could handle the situation. She stared at her reflection in the mirror. Her lips were full and slightly swollen, and was it her imagination, or were her eyes a deeper blue? She wasn't sure she knew this woman who stared back at her.

Parisa was used to being in control of her life. She liked to think caution was her middle name, but what if there was some truth in her deep-rooted fear that maybe she had inherited the reckless nature of so many of her ancestors? She didn't want to believe it, but the fact was that she was in a foreign country, pretending to be engaged to a man she hardly knew and didn't trust. Was that the action of a sensible woman? she asked herself soberly.

Squaring her shoulders, she stood up. The answer was simple. Yes, because the alternative was the ruination of her best friend's future happiness, and Parisa was not prepared to let that happen. Moya was her reason for being here, and if she had any hope of getting through the rest of her stay in Italy she must keep that fact firmly in her mind. It was worth putting up with Luc if it meant her friend could marry Simon with an easy mind.

She turned once more to the wardrobe. She found the matching soft French navy leather high-heeled shoes and slipped them on her feet. She was ready for anything, she told herself sternly, glancing once again at her reflection as she headed for the bedroom door. She decided to go downstairs and explore a little. Anything rather than take the chance that Luc would come back to the bedroom for her.

She stepped into the hall and turned, her blue eyes widening at the sight of Luc walking towards her. He looked magnificent in a black formal dinner suit, the white silk of his shirt contrasting sharply with the sun-tanned bronze of his skin. She felt her heart leap and the colour heightening on her cheeks as his gaze flicked from the pale silver gold of her hair to the blue velvet encasing her shapely form. She instinctively lowered her lashes, hoping to mask the devastating effect he had on her senses from his worldly eyes. Ready for anything, she thought ruefully. Anything, except the potent appeal of Luc Di Maggi...

'Good, you're ready. I was on my way to collect you,' he said smoothly, stopping only inches away from her. His fingers caught her chin, and he tilted her head up, the better to examine her lovely features.

'You look stunningly beautiful, Parisa.' His glance slid down her body and back to her face again, his dark eyes gleaming into hers. 'And you definitely warrant the title "Lady"—a very elegant lady,' he said with quiet sincerity.

'Yes, well, thank you...' she stuttered. Her flesh burned beneath his fingers, and her body was aware of him in every pore. She could not tear her gaze away from his. He was watching her, motionless, as though by the sheer force of his personality he could bend her to his will. She knew he was going to kiss her, and it took all the will-power she possessed to step back and, ignoring the simmering tension, say lightly, 'Shall we go down? Your mother will be expecting us.'

'Coward.' His mouth curled in a knowing smile, but he allowed her to walk past him and down the stairs, although she was conscious all the time that he was only a step behind her, and the hair on the back of her neck stood on end in prickly awareness.

Dinner was an interminable affair, Parisa thought, as she eyed the thousand-layer cake on her plate. She would never be able to eat it. Already she had consumed a fruit juice, a plate of pasta in a Genovese sauce, and Veal alla Marsala. The conversation had been stilted, to say the least. However hard she tried, she could not act naturally with Luc. She told herself it was because she disliked him, and all he stood for, but deep down inside she had a growing suspicion that the opposite was true. She found it so difficult to be natural with him because she was intensely aware of him in a way she had never experienced before. She resented the unaccustomed feelings and consequently responded to him curtly as a form of self-defence.

'Easter wedding is very nice, yes, Parisa.'

'I don't think so.' Parisa answered Signora Di Maggi rather bluntly, but was not quite able to say a flat 'No'. The old lady's delight in the engagement was so obviously genuine, and in other circumstances Parisa couldn't help thinking she would make a lovely mother-in-law. But Parisa was having very little success in keeping up the pretence of a loving fiancée. The subdued elegance of the dining-room, the obvious wealth of the master of the house was in direct contrast to her own shabby home, and she could not get it from her mind that these people were crooks. Luc's mother must be perfectly well aware of how her son made his money, and yet she seemed like any proud mother. The hypocrisy of it—the servants, the fine food and wine all paid for with dirty money. She shot an angry glance at Luc. How was it possible to be attracted to a man—and her own innate honesty forced her to admit he did attract her in the most intense way—and yet know he was outside the law?

Her blue eyes rested on his black downbent head, her expression one of complete bafflement; she didn't understand what was happening to her. She was drawn to him, and yet he was everything she hated in a man.

Luc had been attentive and smiling, but after a particularly caustic comment from Parisa he had given up any pretence of being a loving fiancé. Then, after a brief exchange in Italian with his mother, which Parisa had not understood a word of, he had lapsed into a brooding silence, which was trying Parisa's patience to the limit. It was his stupid idea, and he should have known it would not fool his mother or anyone else, she thought bitterly, and wished she could just get up and walk out.

He lifted his head and looked straight at his mother. '*Scusi, Mamma*. I need to talk to Parisa privately.'

To Parisa's astonishment he upped and walked around the table and caught her arm, muttering, 'Come along to my study.'

She flashed his mother a rather nervous smile as she was hastened out of the door, Luc's arm at her elbow.

'What did you do that for?' she demanded angrily as soon as they were in the hall.

'I need to talk to you. Please don't argue,' Luc said and, opening yet another door off the huge hall, he led her into a book-lined study. 'Sit down,' he commanded tersely, indicating a deep leather buttoned chesterfield beside an elegant marble fireplace.

The fire was lit and the flames danced and flickered in the darkness, until Luc strolled across the room and switched on a table lamp standing on a large carved-oak desk. Even so, the room was not brightly lit. The fire cast eerie shadows on the wall, and as she looked across at Luc his expression was hidden from her by the same shifting shadows.

It was as though he did not want her to see him. She watched as he sat down behind the desk, for all the world as if he were going to conduct a board meeting. She noticed his long fingers pick up a letter-knife, fiddle with it and replace it. He shuffled some papers in front of him. If she had not known better she could have sworn he was nervous.

'So what is so important I could not finish my pudding?' she asked scathingly. The silence in the room was getting to her. She hadn't wanted the fool pudding, in any case.

'You have never had a lover, have you?' he demanded arrogantly, lifting his head to stare across at her.

'What?' Parisa could not believe her ears. He had dragged her from the dining-room to ask that. Her mouth hung open; her blue eyes widened with shock. 'You're crazy,' she finally mumbled, shaking her head.

'No, and you have not answered my question, Parisa.'

'And I'm not bloody well going to,' she said furiously. The nerve of the man!

'You will not swear in my presence,' Luc stated emphatically, striding across the room to lower his large body on to the chesterfield beside her. Her brief defiance vanished and she watched him fearfully, daunted by the determination in his grimly set features.

'But this time I will forgive you. You are right to be afraid of me, Parisa. You do not need to answer. My mother is invariably right, and I can see the answer in your hot cheeks.' His hand brushed lightly down the side of her face and she jerked away from his touch. 'No, stay.' His hand on her arm prevented her getting to her feet.

Parisa shifted warily until she was backed into the corner of the settee. Luc's arm was resting along the back, his other hand holding her wrist in his lap. 'Your mother,' she murmured, completely lost: she did not know what he was talking about.

'Exactly, Parisa.' He grasped the hand that bore his ring, then rubbed the stone, and Parisa felt a flash of guilt at the embarrassment she had caused in the jeweller's, along with a tingling warmth along the length of her arm.

'You and I have a deal, and so far your performance has been woefully inadequate. It wouldn't fool an idiot. At dinner tonight my mother remarked that she was amazed, but glad to note I was showing some respect for my *fidanzata*, because I had not yet taken you to my bed. She could tell you were still a virgin. I looked at you, and somehow my mother's words crystallised in my mind what had been puzzling me all afternoon. She was right. Wasn't she?' he demanded, his fingers tightening on her hand, his dark eyes searching hers.

'Not that it is any business of yours, but yes.' Why shouldn't she admit the truth? She was not ashamed of it. 'It might surprise you to know that in this decade more and more adults prefer a more cautious approach to intimacy to risking the unpleasant and sometimes life-threatening diseases promiscuity encourages,' she said firmly, the glint in her eyes telling him without words that he should try practising a little restraint before it was too late.

'Suppose I told you I am not the promiscuous sex maniac you seem to believe I am, Parisa?'

She arched one delicate eyebrow in disbelief.

'No—and I am the Queen of England,' she said sarcastically. What kind of fool did he take her for? she thought furiously. She had seen him with her own eyes with Margot Mey. He had attempted to blackmail Moya into his bed, and just hours earlier he had tried to get her into bed. The man was a fiend, and she would do well to remember that. Though sitting so close to him, with the musky warmth of his body reaching out to her, it was incredibly difficult.

'I have no intention of arguing with you, Parisa. But I think we'd better get one or two things straight before we go any further.'

' "Straight"—you?' she prompted with a grim smile. 'Don't make me laugh. You don't know the meaning of the word,' she jeered sarcastically.

'That's it,' he snarled, and grabbed her as she would have stood up, and pulled her unceremoniously down on to his lap.

'Let me go!' she demanded, but his arm around her waist kept her pinned against him. He curved one hand around the nape of her neck, holding her head only inches from his darkly furious face.

'Shut up,' he snapped. 'If you want me to keep my side of the bargain, and give you the photographs, you're going to have to do a whole lot better than you have so far. For a start you can cut out the wisecracks,' he declared, his black eyes seeking hers. 'It's up to you. Are you prepared to make some effort to appear a loving fiancée? Or do you want to call the whole thing off with the resultant unfortunate consequences for your friend?' he demanded hardly.

He was much too close, too threatening to argue with.

'No, I want the photographs.' She had no choice and he knew it. She could not disappoint Moya. 'But what exactly do you mean? Am I supposed to hang on your every word?' she couldn't resist sniping.

Stark fury flashed in his black eyes, and his head bent to kiss her hard and angrily. She struggled, trying to break free, while his mouth ground against hers, deliberately hurting her. Then suddenly something odd happened. One second they were fighting, and furious, and the next they were clinging, moulded together in a burning flare of passion.

Parisa lifted her hands, her fingers tangling in the silky black thickness of his hair, and kissed Luc back without even realising what she was doing.

Luc raised his head, his breathing ragged, and they stared at each other, neither one capable of speech. But it was Luc who recovered first.

'Don't look so frightened, Parisa.' His black eyes glittered down into hers. She stared back, her heart racing, her pulse thudding erratically. Her lovely eyes wide and bewildered, she was shocked rigid by her own violent reaction. She couldn't speak.

'I promise I won't do anything without your permission, but, after what has just happened between us, somehow I don't think it will be too difficult to convince a hundred or so very astute people tomorrow night, as well as *Mamma*, that we are a couple, hmm?'

Her eyes fastened on his mouth, but that was a mistake. Her mouth went dry and she flicked the tip of her tongue along her bottom lip in a nervous gesture.

Luc's quick flare of anger appeared to have vanished, as had her own, to be replaced with a fierce sensual awareness she could not control, and that was her second mistake.

She uttered a small, soundless protest as his mouth covered hers again. Reason deserted her and she felt her body weakening against him. His mouth burned against hers, his tongue toying with hers in a sensuous probing dance. Her arms curved around his wide shoulders of their own volition as the kiss went on and on, demanding more. She felt his muscles flex and tense beneath the smooth fabric of his jacket and she yearned to touch him. She slid one hand down over his muscular chest, her fingers inadvertently scratching over the hard male nipple beneath the fine silk shirt.

Luc groaned, breaking the long, passionate kiss, and, drawing away from her, he caught her slender hand and held it firmly against his chest.

'I have my answer, I think,' he said hoarsely, the skin stretched taut across his high cheekbones as he battled with the desire racking his huge frame. 'Now you look as a fiancée should, *cara*.'

Parisa knew the same desire was reflected in her own flushed face. Her eyes, luminous with passion, sought his, and for a second blue and black mingled with an exquisite need. She closed her eyes, unable to sustain the contact. A fierce shudder arced through her. He had won again.

He swung her off his lap and on to the sofa, deliberately moving away from her. 'I think we will take our coffee in here,' he rasped, his breathing irregular. 'My mother does not need that much convincing.'

Luc had wanted her—every instinct told her that—but he had quickly regained his control, while she still burnt with unsated desire. The desire turned to a burning shame in her breast. How could she have behaved so stupidly? And a tiny voice inside her answered that it wasn't hard with such a devastatingly appealing male.

Not looking at him, she ran trembling hands down her skirt. Smoothing it over her knees, she made herself sit up straight, her back rigid. She should have remembered that Luc was a very powerful man, with a cold, arrogant insensitivity. Hadn't she seen for herself the way he turned down his mistress? Parisa had got off lightly.

'The reason I brought you in here was, I want...'

'That is better,' a voice interrupted Luc. It was Signora Di Maggi. 'You two are now friends, no?'

Parisa looked up in surprise, and blushed. 'It is OK. I know the—how do you say?—frustration of young people. My Luc will make you happy; he is much man.'

'*Mamma, prego,*' he said quickly.

Parisa shot a startled glance at Luc, and couldn't stop the smile that curved her full lips. Luc looked decidedly uncomfortable. A first for him, no doubt!

She opened her eyes to bright sunshine and the realisation that someone was knocking on her bedroom door.

'Come in,' she called out. It would be the maid with morning coffee.

'You sound cheerful. You must be a morning person.' Luc's deep voice, tinged with laughter, made her spine tingle.

She grabbed the coverlet up to her chin, her blue eyes wide on his handsome face. 'You! I thought it was the maid.'

'My pleasure, Parisa.' And he walked across to the bed, a laden tray in his large hands. With an economy of movement the tray was placed on the bedside table and the coffee poured, his tanned hand holding out the cup and saucer, before she had gathered her scattered wits.

'Thank you,' she murmured, and took the proffered cup, her colour high at the intimacy of the occasion.

'You look adorable when you blush,' Luc said softly, and she turned bright scarlet. He laughed and winked down at her. 'Don't worry—drink your coffee, and meet

me downstairs in half an hour. I'm taking you out for
the day to avoid the bedlam in the house!'

'Bedlam?' she queried. From what she had seen, his
home was run like clockwork.

'The caterers have arrived, the guest rooms are being
cleaned—the only place to be is out.' And with that he
swung on his heel and left.

Long after he had gone, she held the memory of his
tall, virile figure, casually dressed in blue jeans and a
dark red Pringle sweater, his dark eyes gleaming with
some hidden knowledge she could not quite grasp.
Shaking her hair from her face, she drank the coffee and
ate a croissant before swinging her long legs out of bed,
reminding herself that she had to be on her guard around
Luc at all times. She only had to get through one more
day, and then go home, a return to her own life. It was
that simple.

Standing in front of the long, mirrored door, washed,
and dressed in navy gabardine trousers and a matching
navy and white wool sweater, she brushed her long pale
hair from her face and tied it back with a plain navy
scarf.

Luc could really be quite a charming host, Parisa recognised, remembering last night. After his mother had
joined them in the study, somehow the fierce tension
had evaporated from the room. All three had enjoyed
coffee and tiny chocolate choux cakes. The halting
English of Signora Di Maggi and her obvious en-
thusiasm at their engagement had lightened the atmosphere considerably, so much so that when the old lady
left, after kissing them both good night, they had spent
a surprisingly comfortable hour talking, discussing the
relative merits of Pavarotti and Domingo. Luc was an
opera fan, like most Italians. They had shared a night-
cap. Luc had walked upstairs with her and pressed a soft,
almost brotherly kiss on her forehead, and said, 'A truce,
Parisa, for a day, hmm?' and she had meekly agreed as
he said goodnight with another kiss, outside her door.

Parisa frowned. Luc in a gentle mood was at his most dangerous. Still, she would enjoy her day out, without worrying about the reason for her being here, and, picking up her top coat with one last glance at her reflection, she left the room.

It was like a day out of time, a rare cameo. The sun shone with the first warm rays of the year, etching the landscape in bright, clean colours. Luc drove the Ferrari with an easy expertise along winding country roads. They stood at the top of a gigantic cliff and gloried in the perfect view. The waves crashing against the shore, the screaming of the gulls made a concerto all of their own. At noon they drove down the hill to Portofino.

'This is the best time of the year, I think,' Luc said lazily, helping her out of the car.

'Not the summer?'

'No, in the summer it is full of tourists, the marina is full and the place is very cosmopolitan, but now only the locals are around.' And, as he spoke, a young boy, not more than ten or so, shouted, '*Padrone, padrone,*' and ran towards them. Luc swept the child up in his arms and swung him around, laughing out loud, then gently set the boy down again.

Parisa watched in amazement and then shock. The boy had only one arm. How sad, and yet the small dark face was wreathed in smiles. She did not understand the rapid-fire Italian that passed between the two males, or why Luc gave him money until, as the young boy shot off in the direction of the dock, Luc took her hand in his and explained.

'Paolo is my friend—I pay him to clean my boat for me. I would take you to see it, but I'm hungry.'

Parisa grinned up into his handsome face. 'And nothing must come between you and food,' she joked.

'You could, if you wanted to,' Luc said softly. 'Any time.'

She flushed at the implicit invitation in his dark eyes. 'Let's eat.'

'Still a coward!' And, lifting her hand to his mouth,
he kissed it, and stopped, his fingers tightening. 'Where
is your ring?' he demanded curtly.

'I left it in the bedroom.' She couldn't see that it mat-
tered. 'I wanted to enjoy today as myself,' she explained, sure Luc would understand. 'After all, it's only
costume for the act tonight.'

'If you say so,' Luc responded enigmatically. She
glanced up at him, but he looked past her. For an instant she wondered if she had offended him in some way,
but dismissed the thought as he grinned.

'My favourite restaurant,' he announced, and ushered
her into a small, dark, typically Italian waterside café,
where the proprietor greeted him as an old friend.

Parisa could not remember ever having enjoyed a meal
so much. She had no idea what she was eating, until Lùc
said it was some kind of liver.

'But I hate liver,' she exclaimed, and then laughed as
Luc pointedly glanced at her almost empty plate.

'So I see, *cara*,' he mocked, and refilled her wine glass.

By the time they had finally finished the meal, Parisa
had drunk four glasses of wine to Luc's two.

'Were you trying to get me drunk in there?' she asked
gaily as he led her once more to the car.

'Would I do such a thing? *Me*, the model of de-
corum?' He pointed a finger at his broad chest with a
woefully injured look on his attractive face.

'Yes, but I forgive you,' she chuckled, loving this much
happier easy-going Luc.

Seated in the car, Luc turned to her, his expression
oddly serious.

'You know what I like most about you?'

She looked across at him, surprised and secretly
touched.

'What?' she asked, and her blue eyes were trapped by
the dark gleam in Luc's.

'You don't allow anything to get in the way of your
enjoyment. I blackmailed you into coming here. You

could have made today terrible; instead I've enjoyed every minute. I cannot think of a single one of my acquaintances who would have been so obliging.'

The serious tone and the deepening gleam in his eyes was not something she wanted to recognise; she didn't dare.

'You obviously don't meet the right kind of people,' she said lightly to break the sudden tension, and, turning, she fiddled with her seatbelt.

Luc took it from her and deftly fastened it around her. 'You're probably right, *cara*. But you can judge for yourself tonight.' He started the car and drove off. 'Almost every member of my family and a load of friends are coming to the party.'

Parisa made no reply. His reminder of just why she was in Italy and in his home pretending to be his fiancée was a dampening one. She had almost forgotten his less than savoury character in the delight of the day they had spent together. But now the thought of the evening ahead was a sobering one.

CHAPTER FIVE

PARISA was adding the finishing touch to her make-up. Damn! Her hand holding the lipstick wavered on her top lip, at the knock on the bedroom door.

Quickly blotting her mouth with tissue, she deftly applied the lipstick once again, and, satisfied with the result, she went to answer the door.

The sight of Luc, one arm propped against the door frame, his huge body leaning casually towards her, momentarily robbed her of breath. The jacket of his dinner suit hung open, revealing the white silk shirt pulled taut from his waist diagonally across his massive chest. A quick flush of colour flooded her face, intensifying as his appreciative gaze lazily surveyed her from head to toe, lingering slightly on the soft curve of her full breasts outlined by the strapless black velvet bodice of her gown.

'You look exquisite, Parisa. The dress is definitely you—a touch wild,' he said softly, and gently he lifted her chin. The eyes that looked down into hers were amused and something more she didn't recognise, but it made her pulse race.

She knew the dress was a mistake. 'Wild', he had said—not at all the image she wanted to present. Under her breath she cursed the impulse that had made her buy the evening gown in the closing-down sale of a small boutique in Brighton last year. At the time it had seemed too good a chance to miss. But now, with the wild strawberry taffeta skirt falling in flounces from the neat waist to end above her knees at the front and dipping to mid calf at the back, she realised her mistake.

But reason vanished as he stooped to press his lips against her brow. The kiss was so open and friendly, and yet she felt her body weakening, the musky male scent of him, mingling with some subtle cologne, acted like a powerful aphrodisiac on her senses, one that was to last the whole night through.

His dark velvet voice breathed softly against her ear. 'Ready to join the fray, my sweet fiancée?'

She could not stop the shiver that trembled through her but, gathering her scattered wits, she responded by holding out her hand, the brilliant blue-white stoned ring glittering like fire on her third finger.

'Yes, oh, master, and I have even remembered the prop,' she teased.

Half an hour later, with Luc's arm casually flung around her bare shoulder, his mother at his other side, he said,

'That is about it, ladies. We have greeted everyone, so now I think we can enjoy ourselves. Don't drink too much champagne, *Mamma*,' he teased, before taking Parisa in his arms and whirling her the few steps to the polished dance-floor with all the youthful exuberance of an overgrown schoolboy.

Laughing up at him, Parisa thought she had never seen a more devastatingly handsome man, and tonight he was hers ... Just this once she would throw caution to the wind and enjoy herself, she vowed. A dreamy smile lingered on her soft lips as, with his hand at the base of her spine, and his other hand holding her much smaller one close to his heart, he slanted her an amused, self-satisfied grin before glancing around the elegant, crowded room.

'So far everything has worked perfectly, *cara*. My mother is thoroughly enjoying her birthday; she has never looked happier. At last she can talk endlessly with her cronies at what she thinks is a very real prospect of some grandchildren before long. As for my friends, they are all madly jealous because I have captured such a beautiful lady.' His dark eyes gleamed merrily down at her.

'Don't you feel a tiny bit guilty, Luc, tricking your mother?' Parisa asked with a twinge of shame, wondering for the first time how he would explain the quick ending of the engagement.

For an answer his arm moved and tightened around her slim waist, causing her to come into more intimate contact with his hard body.

'You know exactly how to prick my conscience, Parisa, and yet until a few days ago I would have sworn I didn't have a conscience.'

Tilting her head, she grinned up at him.

'So I am good for something,' she jeered lightly, to hide the chaos he was creating inside her. His long legs rubbed erotically against hers as their bodies moved in perfect unison to the romantic music.

The glittering chandeliers, the band on the raised platform at one end of the elegant room, the people around them all faded into nothing, as his dark, almost black eyes burned down into hers. Parisa blinked, trying to break the spell, and saw a muscle twitch in his cheek.

'You, Parisa, are good for me. Perfect, in fact, and very soon I would like to show you just how perfect we can be together.'

His deep, smoky voice was like a caress against her skin. She knew she should object to the intimacy he was proposing, but her mouth was suddenly dry, her heart beating double speed, and she could feel beneath her fingers the heavy beat of his heart. He pulled her closer, if that were possible, his hand stroking up to her bare back and resting there.

'Relax, Parisa.' Perhaps he had seen something in her eyes. 'We have all the time in the world. It was not my intention to frighten you, *cara*.'

Reassured by his words, and by the unexpected sense of safety she found in his arms, Parisa did relax. Her slender body moved lazily against his in willing compliance as Luc's hand stroked lightly back and forth across her back, toying with her long hair.

His head bent. 'I knew this silk-spun hair would feel as good as it looks,' he breathed huskily against her ear. 'You should always wear it loose, floating around your shoulders like a silver cloud.'

Parisa lifted her head, smiling into his dark, slumberous eyes. 'Not very practical,' she murmured. But she was glad that for once she had given in to the impulse to leave her long hair loose, lifted from her face with two ornate jet combs, a legacy from her great-aunt.

'If you ever cut it, I think I would kill you,' Luc whispered with a strange fierceness that made her glance quickly up at him, catching a wave of dark emotion clouding his eyes. But before she could speak, a voice broke into their private world.

'My turn, Luc; you can't hog the lovely lady all night.'

'Oh, but I can,' Luc responded almost curtly.

The man who had cut in had been introduced to Parisa earlier as Luc's right-hand man, Aldo Gennetti. He was about the height of Parisa, and very good-looking, with black, curly hair and laughing light brown eyes. Beside him stood his wife, one of the loveliest women Parisa had ever seen: very Latin with masses of blue-black hair tumbling down her back, a perfect oval face, huge brown eyes and a wide, full mouth. Anna Gennetti was stunning in a slip of a black dress that plunged to her waist both front and back. A brilliant diamond bracelet that must have cost a bomb circled her slender wrist. In fact Parisa thought the only thing that marred her beauty was the ice in her eyes and the twist of discontent to her mouth.

Anna said something to Luc in rapid Italian and manoeuvred herself between Parisa and Luc. One small red-nailed hand rested on Luc's arm like a talon, and her body pressed against his. Parisa glanced at Luc, and shivered. She hoped Luc never looked at her like that. His eyes were narrowed coldly on the other woman as he replied cynically and in English, 'How can I refuse?'

'Come on, Parisa, it is you and I,' Aldo declared, and Parisa felt herself spun around. 'We will show this lot

how to dance.' The band broke into a quick disco
number, and Parisa thought, Why not? She loved
dancing, and threw herself whole-heartedly into the
pounding beat, gyrating her supple body with a verve
and subtlety few could match; but Aldo was good.

A space cleared around them and in minutes they were
the only couple dancing, the rest content to watch.
Parisa, laughing out loud at Aldo's outrageous compli-
ments as he swung her around on the last note, her long
hair swirling around her shoulders, suddenly caught a
glimpse of Luc's face. He looked furious.

'Thank you, Parisa, you're fantastic,' Aldo said,
fighting to regain his breath.

'Yes, *cara*. I had no idea you were such an exhi-
bitionist,' Luc declared hardly, appearing at her side, his
arm going around her waist and, holding her possess-
ively against him, he bent his dark head, his breath warm
against her cheek. 'In future I would prefer it if you
keep your undoubted talent under control. I do not like
my guests being given a free view of my fiancée's lovely
legs,' he hissed.

She had seen him wrapped around the seductive Anna.
How dared he criticise her? And she wasn't his fiancée,
in any case, she reminded herself, the resentment in her
giving a mutinous set to her small jaw. 'Aren't you forgetting something?' she demanded.

'Shut up, Parisa; do you want the world to hear?' He
spun her against his hard body and whispered the words
against her mouth before he kissed her.

She vaguely heard the cheers but, swaying in Luc's
arms as he ended the kiss, her full lips softly parted, her
dazed eyes staring up into his, she didn't care. One touch,
and she was putty in his hands.

'For tonight at least you are *my Lady* and I will not
tolerate any other man muscling in, understood?' he demanded huskily, pressing a kiss on her brow.

His possessiveness was very flattering, Parisa told
herself, wondering if he could possibly be jealous, and

enormously pleased at the idea. She hugged the thought to herself for the rest of the evening.

They danced again and drank champagne, and Parisa felt like Cinderella at the ball. Luc stayed by her side, a hand at her waist, an arm around her shoulder, acting the loving fiancé to the hilt, until Parisa did not know where pretence ended and reality began, and she didn't care.

Signora Di Maggi left the party around midnight, and after that the guests left in a steady stream, except for four couples who were staying the night. By two in the morning Luc and herself were the only people remaining downstairs.

'Do you want another drink, a night-cap?' he asked huskily, his arm around her waist.

She leaned into his hard strength. 'No.' She yawned. 'It has been a wonderful evening.' She turned shining eyes up to his. 'It seems a shame it has to end, but——'

'No buts, Parisa. It does not have to end, not yet.' She watched his tanned hand pull the bow-tie from his throat, his fingers deftly unfastening the top two buttons of his silk shirt. A *frisson* of excitement shot through with fear tingled down her spine. Just what was he suggesting? She should be insulted!

'I visit the observatory most nights when I am here. Watching the night sky has a somniferous effect on one. How would you like to come with me, hmm...?'

It was not what she had expected, and she felt ashamed of her own wanton presumption. 'Yes, please,' she agreed. Since they had spent a marvellous day together and he had behaved impeccably, it was her own wayward thoughts that were at fault, she told herself sternly.

They crept up the stairs in silence, not wanting to disturb the rest of the house. A concealed door in the panelling around the circular landing led to a narrow flight of stairs. Parisa followed Luc up the dim passageway, a sense of anticipation making her blue eyes sparkle.

'Mind the step,' Luc said softly as he opened the door at the top and stepped down into the room. Parisa followed, taking the hand he offered her in the semi-darkness, a single low-voltage bulb the only light.

She looked around with interest. A large telescope was mounted on a circular dais in the centre of the room. A desk and high leather chair at one side and, at the other, a long, low sofa-bed were the only furnishings.

'It's a bit stark and eerie,' she murmured. The smooth curved walls she found a bit claustrophobic.

'Watch,' Luc commanded, and at a touch of a switch by the door, the domed roof slid apart like a sliced orange to reveal another dome of pure glass and the night sky beyond.

'Oh! It's magical,' she gasped, as Luc extinguished the single light, and the room was illuminated solely by the clear silver light of the moon. She tilted her head back and stared in awe at the star-studded black velvet canopy above.

'We are lucky it is a fine night.' Luc's arm curved around her naked shoulders and, entranced, she walked with him to the centre of the room.

He released her, shrugged off his jacket, and made some adjustment to the telescope. Then, swinging the high chair into position, he sat down and pulled her on to his lap.

'Watch, *cara*.' She did not have to be told. With his strong arm around her waist, his masculine warmth enfolding her, she looked and listened in complete fascination as he pointed out the different stars and constellations.

He was a remarkable man, she thought, her glance straying from the telescope to study his handsome features. He was completely engrossed in the subject, and very knowledgeable. She laid her head against his shoulder, briefly closing her eyes, savouring the moment.

It was as if they were the only two people in the world.
She would remember this night for the rest of her life.

'Sorry, *cara*, I tend to get carried away with my hobby,
and you're tired.' She felt herself lifted in his strong arms.

'Luc...'

He was lowering her on to the long couch, his dark
eyes soft, his sensuous mouth curled in a wry smile.

'Forgive me for a minute. I have to check only one
more, I promise.' And he kissed the tip of her small nose.
'Rest.'

Parisa couldn't answer—or only with a tiny appreciative murmur. She watched him through half-closed eyes
return to his precious telescope, his broad shoulders
tapered to a narrow waist, firm buttocks and long, muscular legs. He was a magnificent male animal, power
and virility in every line of his huge body. She smiled
softly to herself, her eyelashes sweeping her cheeks. She
had seen the respect and deference on the faces of his
friends tonight. He was a large man in every way there
was. His consideration for his mother, and his earlier
concern for the crippled child were testament to his caring
nature.

So why was he a criminal? she thought fuzzily. Perhaps
he had been led into it by others. She wanted to make
excuses for him, she realised, and, however much she
tried to remember he was a blackmailer and a thief, one
glance from those black eyes, and she went weak at the
knees. She smiled. She had never actually believed in
that statement until she had met Luc. 'Weak at the
knees'... Good job she was lying down. Her smile
widened. Too much champagne...

The pad of a finger traced the outline of her mouth
and she drowsily opened her eyes, her lips parting as if
to catch the finger.

'A secret smile, Parisa. What were you thinking?' Luc
was sitting on the edge of the couch, one arm stretched
along the back, supporting his weight as he bent over
her. His other hand dropped from her lips to her throat,

the heel of his hand resting on her breastbone, his fingers stroking gently against her neck.

She felt the gentle caress in every cell in her body. Lazily she smiled into his dark face, and, reaching up, she placed a slender finger over his mouth. 'A gentleman does not ask such a question. A lady has to have some secrets.' She fluttered her long lashes flirtatiously, teasing him.

His answer was to open his mouth over her finger and suck it inside. The hot, slightly abrasive texture of his tongue, the tugging motion seemed to pull directly to the heart of her. She shivered at the intimacy and pulled her hand free, but only because he allowed her to.

'You're cold.' His finger found the pulse that beat madly at her throat, and rested for a moment.

He couldn't be more wrong, she thought, her whole body flushing with heat.

'Let me warm you, Parisa,' he husked.

Her breathing quickening, she reached her slender arms around his shoulders, letting her fingers curl into the black silky hair at the back of his neck, urging him down to her.

'Yes, oh, yes,' she moaned as he covered her face with hot, tiny kisses—her eyes, her cheek. But, avoiding her mouth, he pulled back. Her huge blue eyes fixed on his, a question in their depths.

Luc, in one lithe move, pressed her to the back of the wide sofa, and lay down beside her. His hand slid lower on her chest, his finger following the gentle curve of her breast against the bodice of her dress. His dark eyes glittered black with an intensity of desire, his face taut with the effort to control some emotion.

'Parisa . . . so athletic, and yet you are the most utterly feminine woman I have ever met,' he declared, his breathing laboured. 'Your skin is smoother than the softest silk and as pale as the moonlight. You are my moon goddess. I'm almost afraid to touch you, in case you vanish and I find it is all a dream.'

'If this is a dream I never want to wake up,' Parisa whispered, sliding her small hand underneath the open front of his shirt. She felt him shudder, and then his mouth found hers. His lips, warm and mobile, surprisingly tender, played softly against her mouth, his tongue teasing and then plunging between her parted lips.

Excitement surged through her, making her move against him with a soft murmur of want, her fingers tangling in the curling body hair around a hard male nipple, so that in response his kiss became more demanding, his tongue plunging the darkest recesses of her mouth with insistent increasing passion.

His passion fuelled hers. God; how she wanted him! She reeled with the speed of it all. She was defenceless. His taste was on her lips; he was muscle, heat and urgent need. She strained against him, her free hand curling around the nape of his neck, holding him to her. He growled a low, throaty sound as he pulled his mouth from hers, his lips trailing a line of kisses down her throat and chest.

His fingers found the side zip of her dress, and tugged it down, his mouth hot on her soft flesh. He rasped, 'I have ached to do that all night.' Leaning up, he gently pulled the bodice of her dress down, exposing her naked breast to his view. He stared down at her, and for a second Parisa wanted to cover herself, but then he laid his hands on her swelling breasts and gently squeezed the soft flesh.

Her back arched in involuntary response, and the exquisite sensation made her blood flow heavily through her veins.

'You are perfect,' Luc rasped. 'Firm and slender, but surprisingly voluptuous.' He slid his hands around the soft curves, his thumbs raking across the deep-rose tips, again and again, bringing them to hard, taut peaks of longing.

'Luc,' she breathed, reaching for him, and he lowered his head, his mouth closing over one hard tip, suckling and tasting, until she cried out with the pleasure he aroused.

'I want you, Parisa, I want you...' he grated, his mouth once more finding hers. She trembled, shaking beneath the force of his kiss. He was no longer tender, but urgent with passion. With one hand he swept the dress from her body, his fingers lingering on her naked thigh, and all the time his mouth caused havoc, sweeping from her lips to her breast, nibbling her slender throat. He dragged her hard beneath him, and the force of his arousal shocked her; the rigid heat of it burnt into her belly.

Parisa had never known such emotion. Her body, with a wantonness she had never thought herself capable of, reacted to his every touch. The enticing male scent of him teased and tempted her, and her hands quickly unfastened the remaining buttons of his shirt. She curved her arms around his broad back. Rejoicing in the satin-smooth feel of his hard flesh, with eager fingers she traced the muscle and sinew. He was so male, so much a man, and she ached for him to possess her completely.

'Parisa, Parisa.' He mouthed her name against her throat, and, forcing his head back, he stared down into her passion-hazed eyes.

'If you want to stop, it will have to be——' he groaned as she moved her shapely legs against him '—now.'

She looked into his dark face: the black eyes, their pupils dilated, the sensuous mouth, lips parted, only inches from her own. 'No,' she breathed and, lifting her head, she licked the strong column of his throat.

She felt his muscles lock with tension, then in a moment he had left her. She reached a hand up to him. Surely he could not stop? But as she watched he shrugged off his clothes. She gasped as he stood completely naked, the moonlight bathing his magnificent body in a silver glow. She had never seen a completely naked aroused man in her life, and just for a second she felt a flash of virginal fear, but it vanished, as her fascinated gaze drank in the sight of him. His massive chest rose and fell unevenly, the curling black mat of hair arrowing down over his belly then bushing out between his thighs. She closed her eyes for an instant. He was such a big man towering over her.

But Luc was doing his own survey. 'Parisa, what are you trying to do to me?' he growled. 'Red panties and a garter belt. Are you determined to drive me mad?' Luc slipped his hands in the top of her panties, and slowly removed them, along with the belt and stockings. He tossed them to one side, and slowly stroked his hands back up her legs, her hips, following the indentation of her waist, and once more over her proudly jutting breasts, before he lowered himself over her.

His dark eyes burned down into hers. The touch of his naked body from toe to shoulder was like being struck by lightning: hot, hard, and sizzling. With a little cry she flung her arms around his neck, clinging to him, as he kissed and caressed her smooth flesh in a frenzy of passion. She gasped as his long fingers delved between her thighs, but her legs parted, welcoming his touch at the most sensitive hot, damp core of her.

Her finger-nails dug into his broad shoulders, but she responded helplessly to his groaned demand. 'Touch me, Parisa. I need to know you want me.'

She traced the length of him, her small hand stroking across his thigh, his hard, flat stomach, to the root of his manhood, while all the time the tension built in her loins at his intimate, probing caress.

'*Basta*.' His hand pulled hers away from him, and, sliding between her open thighs, he paused for a moment, supporting himself on his elbows, one either side of her, as her body shook in a paroxysm of pleasure.

'I don't want to hurt you, Parisa, but I might a little.' The skin was pulled taut across his high cheekbones, his lips tight in an effort to retain control. 'I don't think I could bear not to have you now. I have wanted you from the minute I saw you dressed as my own cat burglar.

Beautiful, passionate, strong. God, Parisa!' he groaned. 'What you do to me.' He fumbled with a small packet, but Parisa barely noticed, her eyes fixed on his sensuous mouth.

She was beyond reason; all she knew was that she had to have this man.

'Please, oh please.' Her legs parted wider, trembling, and, as if her plea was the breaking point, Luc slid his hands beneath her buttocks and lifted her up to him.

She cried out as with one swift thrust he broke through the veil of innocence, sheathing himself inside her. She felt an instant of pain as her body stretched to accommodate him. But before she could register the pain Luc was moving again. Slow and deep, he moved against her. She wrapped her legs around him. Her body arched off the couch, her hands clinging to his wide shoulders.

'*Dio*, I can't,' he cried.

She felt him in every fibre of her being as he plunged deeper, hard and fast, surging out of control, and her body instinctively matched his pounding rhythm.

The world tipped on its axis. Parisa's eyes flew open, the night sky a whirling, spinning kaleidoscope of stars—real or imagined, she could not know—as she trembled, her slender body convulsing in mind-shattering turmoil. Luc cried a harsh, deep sound as his huge body was racked with a ferocious response, and, collapsing down on her, he lay, his head resting on her shoulder, the only sound the deep, rasping sound of their breathing.

Their bodies' sweat slick clung together like two halves of a whole. Parisa had never imagined anything could be so perfect, but, being inexperienced, she was not so sure how Luc felt.

'I'm sorry, Parisa. I lost it. Are you OK?' His rasping voice sounded in her ear. 'I never meant to hurt you.'

'Perfect,' she breathed, stretching her limbs along his. 'But what about you?' she murmured shyly.

Luc propped himself up on one elbow and stared down at her in astonishment. '*Dio*! Don't you know? You are everything a man could want.' He kissed her forehead tenderly, brushing a strand of pale hair from her damp brow. 'I knew it would be good between us, but I didn't realise it was possible to be that good. I have never felt that way before, never lost control, only with you, *cara*,' he husked, his breathing slowly returning to normal. 'But I hope to again.'

Her blue eyes glistened as her hand moved to stroke his now rough jaw. 'I never realised——'

'What you were missing.' He chuckled softly.

Closing her eyes, Parisa marvelled at the languorous contentment that had invaded her body. She felt so fulfilled. It seemed so right, lying naked beneath Luc, her legs still entwined with his. So drowsy.

'No regrets, my love?' he demanded throatily.

She couldn't speak. Instead she moved her hands to his broad shoulders, down his sides to the firm buttocks, tracing the magnificent shape of him, so hard, and moist with their loving. Giving him his answer by touch...

His husky laugh echoed in the silence. 'What have I liberated?' he murmured, feathering kisses over her heavy eyelids.

'Hmm,' she sighed, as his lips found hers in the most exquisitely gentle kiss. She felt his great body stirring against her and parted her lips to tease him with her tongue.

'What you do to me,' Luc groaned against her mouth, his hands caressing once more over her breast.

Parisa had not thought anything could be better than the first time, but she was wrong. With the first fiery burst of passion spent, Luc made long, slow love to her, placing small kisses on every inch of her, shaping with his strong hands every curve and plane of her body. Lovingly he stroked and coaxed, leading her deeper into the world of sensory delight until she gave herself completely over to his mastery.

Time was suspended. His dark velvet voice murmured throaty Latin words she did not understand, while, like

a connoisseur of fine wine, Luc savoured her every reaction, but withheld the consummation she was aching
for. Until, finally, she cried out his name, her nails
digging into his broad back, and he came into her again.
Once more he swept her over the edge of ecstasy, and
she was only dimly aware that Luc had followed her into
the same convulsive climax.

Exhausted, she lay under him, still part of him, held
by his hot, damp body. He moved and she had not the
energy to ask why. Then he was lying by her side, pulling
a soft wool rug over them.

'I should let you go, but I can't, not yet,' he groaned.
'My Parisa.' She looked at his handsome face, so close,
not quite realising the enormity of what had happened
and too tired to try. She smiled and nestled against him,
and in seconds was asleep.

CHAPTER SIX

THE ringing of a bell echoing in her head made Parisa blink and reluctantly open her eyes. It was light, and she was staring at the sky. For an instant she did not know where she was, then she felt the hard warmth of a male body as Luc stirred beside her.

'Sorry, Parisa,' he said softly, gently stroking her cheek with the back of his hand before sliding off the couch. 'I have to answer the telephone—it must be urgent. No one would dare disturb me otherwise.' He tucked the rug around her and, unconscious of his nudity, stood up and, scooping up his trousers from where they lay on the floor, he walked across to the desk and picked up the noisy instrument. *'Pronto.'*

She felt bereft, alone on the wide sofa. His casual arrogant comment that no one would dare disturb him somehow made her aware of the ignominy of her position, and the dream she had lived for the past twenty-four hours began to waver. A wary light clouded her blue eyes as she watched him. With the telephone tucked under his black-bristled chin he deftly pulled on his trousers, while listening intently to whoever was on the other end of the line. He was a powerful, dynamic man; even half naked, his presence was awesome. She saw his jaw tighten, a deep frown marking his broad brow. She could not understand what he was saying, but it was obvious that as far as she was concerned he had switched off...

She slowly pulled herself up, leaning against the back of the sofa. She briefly closed her eyes, her face a fiery red as the full enormity of what she had done finally hit her. Keeping the blanket firmly around her, she searched feverishly for her clothes. She didn't bother with her stockings, but slipped her panties on and pulled the evening dress haphazardly over her head. She didn't dare look at Luc. She must have been drunk, mad, bewitched, or all three, she thought helplessly, zipping the side of her dress with a shaking hand.

'Spoil-sport.'

Her head shot up and she winced at the laughing mockery in Luc's dark eyes. Noting her reaction and her burning cheeks, his expression instantly sobered. He snapped out a few curt words, then dropped the telephone and crossed to Parisa. Sweeping her into his strong arms, he held her tight, against his chest.

'No, Parisa, whatever you are thinking it isn't true. Last night we shared something wonderful, and I will not have you ashamed.' He lifted her chin and saw the uncertainty in her huge blue eyes.

'I wanted to make this morning special, Parisa, but unfortunately there is an emergency at the factory in Naples. Apparently there was a fire last night and three men were hurt; I have to leave. But first I have to kiss you.' And, lowering his dark head, he kissed her long and hard. Only when he felt her willing response did he break the kiss and, holding her slightly away, he added masterfully, 'No regrets; I won't allow it.'

A rueful smile pulled at her love-swollen lips. Luc could read her mind so easily that it was scary. 'No, no regrets,' she assured him, and she knew it was true. Whatever happened in the future, Luc had made her a woman in the most wonderful way possible, with care, tenderness and passion, and she could not imagine ever feeling for another man, responding to another man the way she did to Luc. She tried to tell herself it was too quick, it could not be love, but in her heart she knew she loved him . . .

Stunned at what she had discovered, she looked up into his handsome face. Now was not the time to tell him she loved him. She wasn't sure there would ever be a time. But still she smiled—a wide, truly beatific smile, all her new-found love reflected in her brilliant sapphire eyes, clear for him to see.

'Parisa, don't look at me like that,' he groaned. 'I have to leave in half an hour, but you must stay here till I return. We have to talk.'

'When will you be back?' she asked softly.

'A day or two at most.'

She stiffened in his arms. 'But I have to get home. There is Moya...' she said, almost to herself. 'The photographs!' she exclaimed. How could she have forgotten her real reason for being here? Her lover was a blackmailer, perhaps worse! And the light dimmed in her lovely eyes. There was no way she could wait around in Italy for Luc, and her better judgement told her she should complete her task and leave.

'I haven't time to explain so I will let you win this once. I'll get the photographs and arrange for your flight home today, but remember you're mine and wait for my telephone call tonight. Give me your telephone number,' he demanded swiftly.

Some lingering sense of caution made her quote Moya's London number, as Luc took her back to her room.

Dressed once more in navy trousers and a soft wool shirt, Parisa found herself standing at the back of the villa, the incriminating photographs clasped in her hand, and Luc's arm around her shoulders—a very different Luc from the one she had shared the night with. Immaculate in a navy pin-striped three-piece suit, he was the image of the mature, successful male. The helicopter parked on the grass, blades whirring, underscored the image.

'I hate leaving you like this, Parisa, but I must.' Luc stared down at her, his black eyes worried. 'I'll be in London as soon as possible.'

'It's all right, honestly,' she reassured him. 'I understand.' But she didn't. She didn't know the woman she had become. One part of her wanted to cling to Luc,

and her saner mind told her to run and never look back.
He was a crook, albeit a well-dressed one.

'Good girl. That is what I first loved about you—your
loyalty to your friend, and now, I hope, to me,' he said,
oddly serious. 'I know I am a lot older than you and I
should have had more control, but you came to me so
sweetly, I couldn't hold back. I wanted you as I've never
wanted a woman before. Wear my ring and wait for me,
hmm?'

'I will,' she vowed, mesmerised by the tender light in
his black eyes. His words might not have been an outright declaration of love, but they were close enough to
make her heart sing.

He kissed her once again, a brief touch as light as
thistledown on her full lips. 'I will make it up to you. I
promise.' And, hugging her to his hard body one last
time, he ran across the lawn and ducked under the
speeding blades and into the helicopter.

Parisa stood as though turned to stone, a sense of déjà
vu so strong that she couldn't move, and then she remembered. She had heard the words before. 'I will make
it up to you, I promise.' And in her mind's eye she saw
Luc saying the same words to Margot Mey. She had forgotten all about the singer...

On leaden feet she walked back to her bedroom. The
fire was lit and the bedcovers smooth. She wondered if
the maid had noted her bed had not been used. Did it
matter? She shrugged her shoulders, and, crossing to
the fireplace, quite deliberately dropped the packet of
photographs into the flames. Parisa watched them burn.
Mission accomplished, but at what cost to herself...?
She walked into the ornate bathroom, the one that con-
nected to Luc's room. He had quickly showered earlier
and the subtle scent of his cologne still lingered in the
air, achingly familiar.

She moved to the huge bath that only yesterday she
had found decadent, and deliberately turned on the gold
taps. After her behaviour last night, decadence was no

longer a problem, she thought wryly, stripping off her
clothes. Her naked body was reflected over and over
again in the mirrored walls. She stood and stared, as
though studying a stranger. She noted the slight bruises
on her skin, the softer blush marks around her high, full
breasts, where Luc's rough jaw had grazed her tender
flesh, and a great tide of longing surged through her.

Abruptly she turned and stepped into the bath, slowly
lowering herself into the warm water. She turned off the
taps, and lay back. She was over-reacting, she told
herself. So what if Luc had met Margot Mey last
weekend? That was the past. It was possible for a man
to meet a woman and be immediately attracted. God
knew, Parisa thought solemnly, it had happened to her.
Three days in Luc's company and she loved him, so why
couldn't it be the same for Luc? He had told her he
wanted her and his body had certainly reinforced his
statement . . . She rubbed her palms over her wet, aching
breasts, remembering his touch, his mouth . . . She could
not bear to believe he had lied. She would not . . . But
what of the rest? Blackmail!

Parisa picked up a bottle of scented rose oil from an
array of toiletries that lined one side of the bath, and
sprinkled it in the water. Finding a bar of soap, she gently
lathered herself all over. She ached in places and muscles
she had not realised she possessed until last night.
Eventually she stood up, dried herself off with a large,
fluffy mint-green towel, and returned to the bedroom.

Quickly she pulled on clean underwear and stepped
back into her trousers and shirt. She applied a minimum
of make-up to her smooth complexion: a light
moisturiser and a touch of lipgloss. She would wait for
Luc's call; she would not prejudge him. She was
clutching at straws, she knew. But possibly, just possibly,
Moya was the only person he had tried to blackmail.
Maybe Luc had some valid explanation for his criminal
exploits. Who was she kidding? No one but herself. She
had fallen in love with a villain. It was ironic, given her

background, that the one man she could love above all others was a hundred times more reckless than any of her ancestors. At least her family had been reasonably honest, but Luc...

She refused to think about it. Methodically she withdrew her clothes from the wardrobe and packed her suitcase, and, picking it up, along with her top coat, she had one last look around the room. She smiled. The ring was lying where she had dropped it on the dressing table. Luc had told her to wear it, and sliding it back on her finger gave her confidence a boost.

Her confidence took a nosedive an hour later. A buffet breakfast was laid out in the huge formal dining-room. Parisa was standing by the table deciding what to eat, when Tina walked into the room.

'Parisa, you dark horse, why didn't you tell me on Friday that you and Luc were engaged? It's so romantic. Of course, I always suspected he fancied you like mad. He was so furious after that trick we played on him at school, swearing vengeance when usually he would laugh something like that off without a second thought. I'm so pleased for you both.'

She had hardly spoken to Tina last night. The opportunity had never arisen, and this morning she did not feel like listening to the other girl's exuberance over what was, after all, a fake engagement.

'Thank you,' she murmured.

Tina grinned. 'I promised to take some food to Gino; he's waiting in bed.' And with an audacious wink she filled a plate with food and left.

Parisa picked up a plate and placed a croissant on it, and was in the process of pouring out a cup of coffee when Anna, the glamorous brunette, walked in.

'I hear you. You know Luc a long time...' Anna spoke up in fractured English, moving to stand in front of Parisa. 'He give you the ring. He marry you, for his mother.' Her dark eyes, hard as ice, looked spitefully at Parisa. 'His mother. She is pleased. An English Lady.

Luc has given her—how you say?—the status she wanted.'

Parisa turned pale at the other woman's vitriolic comment.

'Be happy now. Luc is not the faithful man. Soon you get the bracelet, like the rest of us...' The bitterness in her tone was frightening, and, holding out her arm, she asked, 'This he gave me. Nice, no...?'

Before Parisa had made sense of the words enough to form a response, Signora Di Maggi appeared and said something that made the other woman turn scarlet and leave the room.

Parisa spent the rest of the morning trying to understand Signora Di Maggi's chattering in a mixture of English and Italian, without much success. She heaved a sigh of relief when the car arrived to take her to the airport and she could finally say goodbye.

'So did you get them? What happened?' Moya demanded.

Parisa dropped her case to the floor.

'You could let me get inside the door before you start with the twenty questions,' she drawled, but the lines of worry etched in Moya's face brought home to her with savage clarity that it was Luc's behaviour that had done this to her friend. How could she love such a man? It went against everything she believed in, and yet in his arms she had forgotten all her scruples in her desperate need for him.

'Your troubles are over, Moya, dear.' She stamped down her own wayward thoughts. 'The photos are burned; I threw them on the fire myself. Now, if you will make me a cup of coffee and then sit down I shall reveal all.'

Ten minutes later she told Moya an abbreviated version of what had occurred, leaving out the more intimate details. The ring she had removed on the plane and it was safely in its box, in her handbag.

'Parisa, I can't begin to tell you how much it means to me. I've been living under the threat of Simon finding out about the photographs for so long, I was beginning to think it would never end. To be honest, when you went off to Italy with the filthy swine I didn't have much hope that the man would finally act honourably. Thank you, Parisa.'

Parisa's lips thinned and she had to bite back an angry retort at Moya's remarks about Luc. Her lovely eyes clouded as she realised Moya's opinion of Luc was probably correct. So why had she, Parisa, made such a fool of herself over him? She had no answer...

The rest of the evening they gossiped about the forthcoming wedding. At least, Moya did. She was leaving her job at the end of the week, and Simon was coming on Sunday to take her to Norfolk to stay with her father until the wedding. But Parisa wasn't really listening. She was waiting for the phone to ring! Finally she arranged to stay with Moya until the weekend, supposedly to go shopping for a bridesmaid's dress. But secretly Parisa hoped Luc would call—or arrive—long before Sunday.

By the time Parisa crawled into bed it was two in the morning, and Luc had still not rung. She lay in the small bed and relived in her mind every word and gesture they had exchanged over the last few days. She could still taste his kisses on her mouth, imagine the wondrous feel of his body, hard against hers. She flushed with remembered heat at the intimacy they had shared, and with a groan of frustration turned over on to her stomach and buried her face in the pillow.

Luc would ring...he must. Perhaps the accident had been more serious than was first thought, she told herself, and he hadn't time to telephone. She suddenly realised she did not even know what kind of factory he owned. What if it were drugs? The questions tormented her. Oh, God! There was no way she could have a relationship with a drug dealer. What was she thinking? Was one crime any worse than another?

She turned restlessly, a thousand different thoughts screaming around her tired mind. A week ago she would have laughed at the idea of herself falling in love, and with a criminal... She had never understood the blind devotion some women gave to their partners, even when they were proven criminals of the worst kind, seeing it as a weakness of character. Now she was beginning to understand the incredible power of love. In Luc's company she saw nothing, felt and wanted only him. Was she falling into the age-old misconception of women through the ages—that the love of a good woman could change a man?

She thought of all the reckless adventures in her own family history, some also outside the law, and the dire warnings from her grandmother about controlling the more extrovert side of her nature. She'd thought she had succeeded until now. Was she being an even bigger fool, waiting for Luc? Finally she fell asleep, still making pathetic excuses for his silence.

By Sunday Parisa had run out of excuses. She had played her part for the past few days, smiling in front of Moya, while crying inside, but now she had to face the fact that Luc was not going to appear or even call. She had to return to Hardcourt Manor and try to put the whole disastrous episode behind her. She had her work, her home, and David. Luc was a villain and he had used her. End of story... But nothing could assuage the ache in her heart and the dreadful sense of loss.

Parisa sat morosely at the breakfast table, sipping a cup of coffee. Her bag was packed.

'Parisa, look at this,' Moya exclaimed, shoving the Sunday paper in front of her on the table. 'The slimeball has been caught.'

She glanced at where Moya was pointing, and all the colour drained from Parisa's face. Luc arrested! There was a picture of Luc, but her friend's finger was firmly placed on the picture next to it of another man. Heart racing, she began to read.

She couldn't believe it... It was too incredible... Luca Di Maggi, one of the wealthiest entrepreneurs in Europe, had last week acquired, as part of a large property company he had taken over, the ownership of a London casino. His first act as the new owner had been to fire the casino manager and report his fraud to the police—on Thursday Luigi Reno had been arrested on fraud charges amounting to thousands of pounds.

'Is that the man who——?' Parisa asked Moya unsteadily, pointing to the ferret-faced man next to Luc's picture.

'You know it is, Parisa. The police must have picked him up as soon as he came back to England.'

Parisa started to laugh hysterically; she couldn't help it. She had gone to Italy with the wrong man...

Simon arrived, and before Parisa had time to think about the enormity of her discovery she was hustled out of the flat and into the car. Simon was in a hurry to drop her off at the railway station and carry on to Norfolk with Moya.

An hour later she was alone on the train. Her bright façade crumbled and moisture filled her large eyes as she read the newspaper article once more. There was quite a write-up about Luc. Apparently he had started life as the son of a small village baker, and on the death of his father had expanded this business into a string of bakeries and then a chain of pizza houses that flourished on four continents. Not content with that, he had diversified into shipping and property, and was now the sole owner of a world-wide company.

Parisa's relief at discovering Luc was not a crook was quickly followed by despair. When she had thought he was a small-time crook, she might just have got over him; her distaste for his occupation would eventually have killed her love for him. But knowing he was a multi-millionaire who had quite deliberately seduced her hurt more than she could bear.

What a fool she had been, imagining for one minute that a mature sophisticated man like Luc could possibly fall in love with her. She was as naïve as the fourteen-year-old she had been when she first met him, she realised sadly. It was the only explanation for her stupidity. His villa, the jet, his glamorous friends...all screamed wealth. She should have guessed... But life so far had not prepared her for mixing in the jet-set world that Luc obviously inhabited.

She had all the social graces: her parents, then boarding-school had taught her well. But her late teens had been spent training for the Olympics with no time for the boyfriends most girls of her age enjoyed. When her rowing career ended she had gone straight into teaching sport at a private school. Her home life, living in the manor house with an elderly couple, suited her: she was and always would be a country girl at heart. No match for the sophisticated Luca Di Maggi.

She had fallen like a ripe plum into his arms, giving him everything, and all the time it had been a game to him. First he had tricked her into going to Italy. In fact he had blackmailed her! The photographs might have been taken by another man. But it had been Luc who had used them to blackmail Parisa. He must have thought it was a huge joke. All the time in Italy, while she had been worried sick for her friend, he had been laughing up his sleeve.

Margot Mey had named him well—a master of passion, once Parisa was in his home, with his elderly parent delighted by her presence. She had succumbed to his overpowering masculine charm with a naïve simplicity he must have thought hilarious. It was her own fault: she had agreed to stay in Italy and deceive everyone at the birthday party. But Luc had carried the deception further. He had made love to her without restraint, knowing full well he had no intention of ever seeing her again. Five days she had stayed in London with Moya, and if she was honest she had spent every minute of every day hoping he would call or arrive. He had never had any intention of calling, she realised now. He had probably taken her to bed to get back at her for the trick she had played on him in the boat-house, nothing more...

Suddenly his behaviour when he had found Parisa in the apartment made sense. She remembered thinking he had seemed puzzled and he had said, 'You think I am blackmailing this girl,' and she had accused him of playing games... In a way she had been right. It hadn't taken the man a second to realise what had happened and turn it to his own advantage. He had got a fake fiancée with impeccable pedigree to please his mother as well as getting his revenge on Parisa for embarrassing him years earlier. Tina, his own cousin, had mentioned that Luc had vowed vengeance at the time.

The hurt was like a knife in her stomach. She felt nauseous at the thought of her own wanton response to his lovemaking, while he had been fully in control. She had been flattered to think he had protected her against pregnancy, but now she realised it was himself he had been protecting. She had even asked him if it was all right for him... What a joke! No wonder he had made no objection when she'd said she had to return to England. He probably couldn't get her flight booked fast enough.

A hollow laugh escaped her. 'Wear my ring', he had said. A fake jewel for a fake love-affair was somehow very appropriate. No, not a love-affair, she told herself with bitter honesty. A one-night stand... That was all she had ever been to him.

She rubbed a tired hand across her damp eyes. In one week Luc Di Maggi had turned her into the impulsive person she had vowed never to be. Had he told her the truth about anything? she wondered. It was quite possible, in fact, probable, that there never was an accident in Naples. The phone call could have been about anything. Parisa didn't speak Italian. Luc could lie to her with no fear of being found out.

By the time Parisa finally entered the front door of Hardcourt Manor her grief was slowly turning to icy anger. So she had been a fool. But no more. Tomorrow she was back at school and she was going to get straight on to her solicitor to see what could be done about the financial state of the manor. She was back to reality and the rigours of everyday living and never again would she allow her emotions to overrule her common sense.

Parisa drove the old beaten-up Beetle with exaggerated care through Brighton's lunch-hour traffic and out on to the open road. She barely noticed as she spun through Hailsham and the small village of Magum Down. In the two months since her return from Italy she felt as though she had aged ten years. But today she felt good. Walking into the bank and depositing a cheque for sixty thousand pounds would do it every time, she thought happily.

At last something seemed to be going right in her life. God knew she could do with a change of luck, after the agony of the past weeks. She had forced herself to carry on as normal and had even accepted a couple of dates with David, but she had known she wasn't being fair to him and had finally told him they could only ever be friends.

She had returned to work the day after returning from London, a sadder and wiser woman. She had been forced to accept the unpleasant truth that Luc had no intention of ever seeing her again. All his fine words had been no more than that: just words. She had behaved like the impulsive woman Luc had called her, and that alone had almost destroyed her self-confidence.

The only good thing in those early weeks was that Mr Jarvis had finally found a way for her to make money. It was quite simple. Parisa could not sell the manor house, and the existing covenant stated it could not be converted to an inn or such like. But Mr Jarvis had dis-

covered she could sell the title 'Lord of the Manor of
Hardcourt'. Seemingly a law had been passed in 1922
that allowed the title to be divorced from the property,
and Parisa could legally sell the lordship of the manor
without actually selling the house. Mr Jarvis had contacted Sotheby's and they had given him the name of a
London-based estate agent and valuer who were quite
happy to handle the sale.

Four weeks later Parisa had gone up to Norfolk for
the wedding. She had pinned a smile on her face and
acted the happy bridesmaid. Oddly enough, from then
on she had begun to recover. Perhaps it was seeing Moya
so happy. It had made her realise life went on. She had
made one ghastly mistake. She was not the first girl to
be fooled by a charming rogue of a man, and she certainly wouldn't be the last, but wallowing in self-pity
was self-destructive. Plus, when she returned home, Mr
Jarvis had called her with the news that a buyer had
been found for the title.

Parisa smiled slightly as she manoeuvred the car round
a tight bend. Didi had hated the idea, and advised
strongly against it, but Parisa had done it anyway. She
was still quite bemused at how easy it had been.
Seemingly some foreigners would pay quite fantastic
sums for the title 'Lord of the Manor'. Thank God! she
said silently. Her troubles were almost over; at least now
she could make a start on the more vital repairs to the
house, and hopefully provide Didi and Joe with some
kind of security in their old age.

Didi she would have to handle delicately; the old lady
had never stopped nagging her since the prospect was
first mentioned. Well, it was done now, and Didi would
have to lump it... School had ended last Friday for the
Easter break and today, Monday, Parisa had met her
solicitor to conclude the transaction. Her heart felt
lighter; at last she was beginning to get her life in order
again...

A car horn broke into her musing, and, grasping the wheel firmly, she brought her full attention to the road ahead until she arrived at Hardcourt Manor.

With a smile tilting her full lips, Parisa dashed into the house. 'Didi, good news!' she cried, shrugging out of her short car coat and dropping it and her bag on a convenient chair.

The housekeeper walked slowly from the sitting-room. 'Yes, later, Miss Parisa, but first——'

'No, listen, Didi. I've seen Mr Jarvis, and the deed is done and the cheque is in the bank.' She paused for breath, and also because she was not sure how Didi would take what she had said.

'Never mind that old fool, girl. But why——'

Parisa, getting her second wind, cut in. 'Sixty thousand, Didi. Just think—we can have a new roof.'

'Impulsive as ever, Parisa, darling.' The deep, mockingly familiar voice sounded in her head.

Parisa shook her head. God, was she hearing voices now? She looked across the top of Didi's grey curls, and froze. Outlined in the sitting-room door, the light behind him masking his features, was the tall—very tall—figure of a man.

'That is what I was trying to tell you, Miss Parisa,' Didi said disgustedly. 'Your fiancé arrived hours ago, and I do think you might have told me. I didn't know what Master Luc was talking about at first. It was only after he explained about the holiday and I remembered seeing that lovely ring that I realised Luc was telling the truth, and then the telephone has never stopped ringing all day.'

'He told you we're engaged?' Parisa could not believe what she was hearing.

'Yes, and you should have done so. Hmph! Engaged to be married, and not once did you tell your old nanny, but then I'm just a servant around here. Who takes any notice of me? I was horrified at the idea of your selling the title; you could have told me who was buying it and saved me all that worry.' Parisa silently groaned. Didi was upset. 'Thank goodness your fiancé is more open about his dealings than you are. I'm going to make a pot of tea. You can answer the telephone yourself.' And, still muttering, she left.

Parisa, barely registering Didi's words, clutched the hall table with one hand, to help support her trembling legs. Luc, casually dressed in a black leather blouson jacket hanging open to reveal a white roll-necked cashmere sweater, a lean waist and belted black pleated trousers, was striding towards her. For a second she had the wild thought that she had conjured him up out of her imagination, but as she bravely looked up into his handsome face she knew he was all too real. Blue eyes locked with black, and for a long moment there was complete silence.

It was Luc, but a different image to the one she remembered. He was thinner, his handsome face gaunt, and his bronzed skin held a greyish tinge. His clothes hung loose on his huge frame, and his hair... his beautiful, thick, glossy black hair that she had delighted in running her fingers through...

'What happened to your hair?' she exclaimed involuntarily. It was cropped short, a dark, barely inch-long stubble over his arrogant head.

'I had it cut,' he said flatly. 'But you must have realised it would be.'

'What?' She did not know what he was talking about, and, tearing her gaze away from his, she forced her chaotic emotions under some kind of control. He was here in her home, and what had Didi said? Her *fiancé*. The swine had told Didi they were engaged.

'How dare you come into my home and tell my housekeeper an outright lie? We are not engaged and never have been. I'm afraid I must ask you to leave.' And, with a regal if somewhat dramatic gesture, she indicated the front door, silently amazed that her voice sounded cool and authoritative, even as her mind spun in crazy disbelief at Luc's presence.

'You did that very well, Parisa. Every inch the Lady of the Manor,' he drawled cynically. 'What a shame the title is no longer yours.'

He must have heard what she had told Didi! 'My personal affairs are hardly your concern, Mr Di Maggi,' she said with an arrogantly arched eyebrow.

'As I was your first personal affair only weeks ago I think I am entitled to be curious.'

Parisa turned scarlet in the face of his open reference to the night they had spent together. Her blue eyes clashed with glittering black and she wanted to throw good manners to the wind and scream at the man to get out, and he knew it. She could see it in the taunting, cynical smile as he glanced at her small hands clenched around the edge of the table.

'A one-night stand does not constitute an affair,' she said bitingly. 'And if you were anything of a gentleman——'

'But then you never thought of me as a gentleman, did you, Parisa? You considered me as some kind of low-life,' he snarled, his temper showing. 'What was it, Parisa? The hooray Henries not men enough for you? You fancied a bit of rough for your initiation? Or perhaps it was the ring you wanted to hang on to. Obviously you needed the money.'

'How dare you come to my home...?' She was livid. She had waited in London five days for his call, and now, two months later, he had sauntered back into her life and had the gall to suggest she had slept with him for the sake of a bit of costume jewellery.

'Tea, Miss Parisa.' Didi walked into the hall pushing an antique wooden trolley loaded with the best family china and the silver tea service, plus a plate of home-made biscuits.

Parisa was silenced by the old lady's interruption, but the ring of the telephone, only inches from her hand on the hall table, made her jump. Automatically she picked up the receiver.

Her pale face turned scarlet and back to white in a few seconds, as she listened in horror to the ravings of a demented David, who had just read the announcement of her engagement in *The Times*.

'You could have told me. I deserved better than that, Parisa. No wonder you said we could only ever be friends when I was going to ask you to marry me. How could you? But then the man is filthy rich——'

'You were going to marry me?' Parisa parroted, and turned scarlet as a nasty swear-word echoed down the line as the receiver was replaced at the other end. She swung around, blue eyes flashing dangerously, but the object of her anger was disappearing into the drawing-room opposite. Parisa stormed after Luc. 'Just what the . . . ?' She stopped. Luc had sat down in a large, shabby, wing-backed chair and was smiling benignly at Didi, as the old lady proceeded to pour out two cups of tea.

'Sit down, Miss Parisa, and enjoy your tea. I know you and Mr Luc must have lots to catch up on.'

'Thank you, Didi,' Luc responded smoothly.

Parisa's mouth hung open in shock. Nobody called Mrs Trimble 'Didi' except herself, and she could not believe Luc had charmed the old lady so quickly, but one look at Didi's simpering smile and she knew yet another woman had fallen for Luc's distinctive charm.

'My pleasure, sir.' And, handing him a cup of tea, she turned to Parisa. 'After tea——' she held out the cup and saucer and Parisa automatically took it '—why don't you show Mr Luc around the house and tell him the history? As the new Lord of Hardcourt Manor, it will be fascinating for him.'

'That was David on the telephone, and he is . . .' Then what Didi had said registered through her anger. 'The new Lord! Oh, my God!' she exclaimed. She collapsed on the sofa and gulped down the tea, almost burning her mouth. The shock of Luc's unexpected arrival had thrown her thoughts into complete confusion. Half an hour ago she had been congratulating herself on finally beginning to get over him, on getting her life back in gear, and now... A horrible sinking sensation settled in her stomach. She had signed the title over to a company. What had Jarvis said? The company had bought it intending to use the coat of arms on the letterheadings or something. Could it possibly be Luc's...?

'Yes. You're right, Parisa.' He read her mind again.

In her own home, with generations of history to back her up, she responded with cool hauteur. 'You may have bought the title, but your lawyer should have explained that it does not give you the right to visit this house.'

'Miss Parisa, remember your manners,' Didi scolded.

Parisa could feel the anger building inside her, but she forced herself to stay calm, to think, and slowly, as she drained her cup, she began to get her thoughts into some kind of order. It infuriated her to think the sixty-thousand-pound cheque she had been ecstatic about a couple of hours ago had come from Luc. So what if his company had bought the title? It was nothing to do with her, she tried to tell herself. As far as she was concerned it was just a useless bit of parchment that, by selling, meant she was able to struggle on a bit longer in her old home. There were other such houses dotted around the country, the owners left with little money and great mansions that only the incredibly wealthy could maintain. Some were changed to hotels or retirement homes, but she had not had that option.

But why Luc had called was a mystery. And why claim he was her fiancé and tell the world in *The Times* newspaper? What machiavellian scheme was he plotting now? she asked herself warily. Surreptitiously, she studied him beneath lowered lashes. His long body was casually at ease in what had been her father's favourite chair, his dark eyes smiling at Didi as he accepted a biscuit from the plate she was proffering. Parisa was caught once again by the sheer animal magnetism of the man.

Once he had smiled at *her* that way, and pain, unexpected and quite devastating, hit her. Her stomach churned and for a second she thought she was going to be physically sick. Whatever he wanted, it didn't matter. She wanted him out of her house, out of her sight, out of her life . . . She despised him . . .

With a supreme effort of self-control she finally responded to Didi's prompting. 'Actually, the house is not very interesting, and I'm sure Luc has to get back to London,' she said politely, bravely raising her eyes to meet his. 'It was nice of you to call, but don't let me delay you,' she concluded with dry sarcasm.

But Luc was not so easily dismissed, and Didi's parting comment was no help. 'Now, Miss Parisa, that's no way to talk to the man you are going to marry. I've booked a table for the two of you at the Old Forge for dinner. Remember, this is my bingo night, so if you don't mind I'll go and get ready.'

CHAPTER SEVEN

PARISA'S temper boiled over as soon as Didi closed the door behind her. 'What the hell do you think you're playing at?' She jumped to her feet, her face pale, her slender body shaking with the force of her anger. 'Coming into my home, telling my housekeeper you are the new Lord of Hardcourt and my fiancé. What kind of fable is that?' she raged.

'No fable. The announcement of our engagement was in this morning's *Times* and I am Savion Holdings. By a strange coincidence, the estate agent you used to sell the title happens to be part of the property company I recently acquired. When I saw the name Hardcourt I couldn't resist the temptation and purchased the title. It seemed rather fitting, I thought.'

It was true; she could tell by the triumphant glitter in his black eyes. But what about the rest? 'David... The papers...' she spluttered. Suddenly the enormity of what Luc had done hit her. Oh, my God! She realised everyone in the county would know.

She had no idea how magnificent she looked, standing in the middle of the room, her blue eyes flashing fire, the soft red wool-knit dress she wore clinging to every curve of her slender form.

'*Dio*! You have the face of an angel, the body of a temptress, and a heart as hard as nails.' Luc's deep voice cut into the tense silence.

Parisa flushed scarlet, then paled at his final comment. If anyone had a heart as hard as nails it was Luc, she thought bitterly. But before she could open her mouth to repudiate him, he had got to his feet and covered the distance between them. He grabbed her by her shoulders. She stiffened, shooting a furious glance at his dark countenance, and seething at the arrogant contempt she saw in his black eyes.

His cold, cynical gaze roamed her infuriated face. 'Your poor sod of a boyfriend is well rid of you. Did you bother to tell him you had already been in my bed?' She flushed even brighter. 'No. I thought not.' His sensuous mouth curved in a hard sneer. 'It is time you faced up to your selfish actions, and I am going to make sure you do.'

He was much too close. His aggressive masculinity threatened her in ways she refused to admit, but his words incited her fury. How dared he call her selfish, the swine? And, without thinking, she raised her hand to strike him. But her arm was caught in mid air, and with embarrassing ease Luc twisted it behind her back, hauling her tight against his huge frame.

The anger, the tension crackled between them like an electric storm. Her breasts were flattened against his broad chest. Her mouth opened to demand her release, but she never uttered a word. His hand slid from her shoulder to tangle in her long hair, tightening till the pain almost made her cry out, but his mouth silenced her, grinding against hers in a savage, bruising assault. She could not believe it was happening. The rage, the pent-up violence in the thrusting force of his kiss was shocking in its intensity, and to her horror all her fight deserted her as she went limp in his arms.

He released her so abruptly that she almost fell. Her tongue licked involuntarily over her swollen lips. Her head still tilted back, she stared numbly up at Luc, too shocked to speak.

'Don't ever raise your hand to me again, Parisa.' His face grey beneath his tan, his black eyes sliced into her. 'I have no desire to hurt you. That is not why I'm here.'

He could have fooled her! she thought, the painful throbbing of her lips all too real. He turned and walked across the room. She stared at his broad back, the tightness of his wide shoulders, too stunned by the explosion of raw passion to move.

'Then why?' she asked, fighting to regain control of her chaotic emotions. She didn't understand; her brain just would not function. Her legs trembling, she sank back down on the sofa, closing her eyes for a moment. It had to be a nightmare. Any second now she would wake and her life would be back to normal. Slowly she opened her eyes, but it wasn't so. Luc had moved and was now standing with one arm leaning against the ornate oak-carved fireplace, his interested gaze roaming around the room and finally settling on Parisa.

'I can see why you need money, Parisa. It's a lovely old house, but it does need cash spending on it. I'm surprised you can afford an apartment in the city, but then a London address must be convenient for you to hand out to unwanted friends...' he prompted cynically.

'Something like that,' she snapped. 'But it obviously didn't work in your case.'

'Liar. It isn't your apartment. It belongs to your friend Moya.'

'So what?' Suddenly she remembered the day they bought the ring. No wonder he had insisted on driving her home to find out her address . . . the original blackmailer knew where Moya lived. What an idiot she had been not to realise it at the time, and she could have spared herself an awful lot of heartache. 'You wouldn't be here if I hadn't put the title up for sale.' She unconsciously spoke her thoughts out loud.

'Is that your idea of an explanation for your actions?' Luc laughed—a harsh, humourless sound.

'I don't owe you an explanation,' Parisa said bluntly. It was the other way around, she thought mutinously. But a tiny flicker of something very like hope stirred in her breast. How had Luc discovered the apartment was not hers, unless he had called there looking for her? But immediately she squashed the feeling. Yes, but weeks later, she told herself cynically, and, shooting Luc a poisonous glance, she demanded, 'You have yet to explain why you are here, and the ridiculous assumption that I am your fiancée.'

'Not assumption. Fact, Parisa, and you have a very expensive ring to prove it.'

'That bauble served its purpose for you.' She responded with icy politeness to cover her deep resentment. He had certainly got his money's worth out of that piece of costume jewellery in the two days they had spent together in Italy.

'I would hardly call a brilliant blue-white diamond a bauble. You were good in bed, but not that good, and I am not in the habit of paying out a small fortune for a one-night stand,' he drawled mockingly. His black eyes caught and held hers, and she could not hide the shock his words had caused her.

He was saying the stone was real. She couldn't believe it—a brilliant blue-white, she knew, was one of the most expensive diamonds in the world.

'I'm surprised you haven't sold it as you need money so badly. Or have you?' Luc's cynical query made her stiffen in her seat.

'No,' she snapped, still digesting his other comment. He had not found making love to her much good! Why did that hurt? She had realised weeks ago that Luc had obviously not been as bowled over by the one night of passion they had shared as she herself had. What had been the most marvellous experience of her life had been just sex to him. She raised her head, and with a curious detachment surveyed the man leaning negligently against the fireplace as though he were a total stranger. But her attention was caught as he pushed one hand into the pocket of his elegant black trousers, pulling the fine wool cloth over his powerful thigh. She turned her head defensively. There was no mistaking his virile masculine appeal. It radiated from every line of his large body, but she refused to acknowledge that he could still affect her.

Luc didn't make love to women; the word wasn't in his vocabulary. He hadn't made love to Parisa. He had practised his mastery of the sexual act, nothing more. He had used her for amusement in revenge for a childish prank. He had covered it with sweet talk and a semblance of caring, which only made it worse. Now the final insult—he thought he had paid far too much for the privilege. Hadn't he just said so...?

'What do you want, Luc?' she said flatly. 'The ring back?' She got to her feet, her blue gaze remote on his still figure. Every inch the lady, she walked, head high, towards the door. 'I'll get it for you and then you can go.'

'No. Stay.' His curt command stopped her. She turned with her hand on the doorknob.

'There is something more?' she queried with icy politeness. 'You do surprise me. You already own the title of the manor, but the house is not for sale. You and your mother will have to content yourself with a piece of paper and a coat of arms.' And much good may it do the pair of them, she thought bitterly. Anna Gennetti had been right. The Di Maggis were status seekers, something she could not abide.

Puzzlement then anger flashed in his dark eyes, as the impact of her words struck home. He searched her cool, composed features, his glance skimming insultingly over her rigidly held body, lingering for an instant on the firm outline of her breasts, before returning to her face. It took all her self-control to hold his gaze without blushing. Anticipating his furious response, she was mystified as his saturnine features resolved into a bland mask to match her own.

'My mother is in the Royal Free Hospital in London. She thinks we are engaged.' His tone remote, Luc continued, 'I promised I would take you to visit her. I had the announcement printed in *The Times* simply as an alternative if I did not find you at home. I considered the formal announcement would be some reassurance for *Mamma*. She is very ill and I do not want her upset or worried.'

So that was it... Instantly, Parisa believed him. Of course, it made sense. Why else would he bother tracking her down? Certainly not because he had any feelings for her. He had made that very plain...

'I'm sorry about your mother. What's wrong?' she asked courteously. It was as though an invisible barrier had slid between them. They spoke as two polite strangers, and that suited Parisa perfectly.

'She had a slight heart attack a few weeks ago. On Thursday she is to undergo a bypass operation.'

'I see.'

'Enough to come with me to visit her tomorrow?'

Parisa was sorry Signora Di Maggi was ill, but she had no intention of getting involved with Luc or his family again; once was quite enough. 'Yes, well, I'm afraid I can't,' she said coolly.

Luc straightened. 'You owe me... and I collect on my debts.' His dark eyes burned with a deep-seated anger as he moved purposefully towards her.

Parisa turned the door-handle, intent on escape, but was foiled as Didi entered.

'I thought I'd better tell you.' The elderly lady smiled at Luc. 'Your chauffeur has returned and he is waiting in the kitchen.' So now she knew, Parisa thought, why she had never seen a car in the drive when she had arrived home. 'And I've booked your table for seven,' Didi continued, turning her attention to Parisa. 'That will give you plenty of time to show Mr Luc around the house. Tomorrow, when you go to visit his mother——'

'Didi, I'm not going to dinner or to London——'

'Rubbish, girl, of course you are. You can't let Master Luc and your future mother-in-law down.'

'But...' Parisa should have known after a lifetime with Didi that there was no way she was going to win this particular argument. Ten minutes later she was pointing out the various portraits in the large entrance hall and then leading Luc up the wide staircase, still wondering how it had happened. 'Mind the carpet,' she said automatically as they reached the worn part.

She stopped in front of a massive oil-painting in an ornate gilt frame, and turned as Luc stood by her side. 'Hardcourts have lived here since the twelfth century. The local baron gave the manorial rights to an ancient ancestor, for fighting for him—there was no such thing as pay in those days. The house has been rebuilt over the centuries, the last time in 1850. This is Lady Penelope, one of the earliest portraits.' It was a picture of a woman in seventeenth-century clothes, who looked rather like Parisa, with the same distinctive white-blonde hair.

'Her husband was a sea captain, and died at sea. Rumour has it he was actually a pirate. She was left with a baby daughter and the house. In those days it would have passed to the next male in the family, but as it happened the next male was a distant relative, who was an earl in his own right. He very graciously allowed the entail to be altered so the property could be passed to the first-born child of the family, irrespective of sex. A very unusual entail in those times, and the manor has passed down through both the male and female line ever since. That is why some of the portraits bear different hyphenated names, the only constant being the Hardcourt.' She sounded like a tour guide, but didn't care.

'Interesting. I did wonder why the surname on the portraits varied.'

'Yes, it is quite unusual.'

'She was very lovely; you look rather like her.' Luc turned his head, glancing down at her.

Parisa felt the colour rise in her cheeks. He was much too close and, to her chagrin, her intense awareness of him was suddenly rekindled. But then it was his nature to flirt with anything in a skirt, she told herself firmly.

'It was lucky the house was entailed so progressively. It has been the curse of the Hardcourt men to get themselves killed in a haphazard fashion.' She pointed at the next portrait, of an elegantly dressed Regency buck. 'Hubert Hardcourt. He was on a tiger hunt in India, and was eaten by the beast he set out to trap. The next male member of the family managed to get lost in Africa. And as for the women,' she went on, 'they all seem to marry rogues and adventurers.' She moved along, pointing to yet another portrait of a lady, who was dressed in nineteen-twenties style.

'Even the women who didn't marry had a propensity for getting into hot water. This one, Patricia, tied herself to the railings outside Downing Street. She was a suffragette and ended up in gaol. Though to give her her due, after her brother was killed in the First World War and his wife died, she was left in charge of a nephew and niece, and before the young Hardcourt of the day managed to get his hands on what was left of the family fortune she had a trust set up for the maintenance of the manor. Unfortunately the covenant attached insists it must remain a family home.'

'That explains a lot,' Luc said with a chuckle.

Parisa looked up at him, not in the least amused. When she was a small child her grandmother, a thoroughly sensible lady, and not a Hardcourt by birth, had told her all the family history. Then it hadn't bothered Parisa that her ancestors were impulsive and prone to crazy adventures. She had loved her parents, and her mother had been as adventurous as the man she married. Consequently, as a child Parisa had often been left behind, while they set off on some crazy escapade. She had never been conscious of it worrying her until after their death. Then her grandmother had made a point of impressing on her how important it was not to get involved in reckless escapades as her parents had. She had a duty to look after the manor and its inhabitants. When she lost her grandmother as well, Parisa had consciously tried to squash the more extrovert side of her personality, seeing it as an inherited flaw in her nature. Now she disliked the least hint that she was impulsive or prone to reckless acts.

'I do not find it funny,' she said bluntly. 'If any of them had had the least bit of business sense, I wouldn't be stuck with this huge house I can't sell and I can't afford to keep.'

'What happened to the trust?' he queried.

'A few thousand may have seemed a lot in the nineteen-twenties, but today the income from it just about covers the wages of Didi and Joe, but only because they work for next to nothing. As for the house, the original entail forbids it being sold and the covenant forbids it being used for business.'

'Surely the covenant could be broken?'

'Don't think I haven't tried. With twelve bedrooms, if I could turn it into a guest-house or something it might pay, but Mr Jarvis informed me it isn't possible. But now, thanks to you and your status seeking,' she sniped sarcastically, 'I will be able to repair the roof and maybe the heating.'

Luc, ignoring her sarcasm, responded in a businesslike tone, 'That's not a long-term solution, Parisa. Take it from me—it will cost double what I've paid you for running repairs alone.' He caught her arm, and she flinched. Something sinister flickered in his dark eyes, but his hand dropped abruptly from her arm.

'It really isn't any of your business.' She moved away. She hated to admit it, but he was probably right about the money and repairs as well...

'Oh, I don't know. As the new Lord——'

'You may own the title, but you'll never be my lord and master, whatever you told Didi,' she snapped.

'Who said I wanted to be?' he queried silkily. 'As for Didi, presenting her with a red garter belt was proof enough for the lady that you and I were involved.' And with a casual glance at his watch he added, 'It's almost six. Do you want to freshen up?'

Blushing as scarlet as the damned belt he had mentioned, she said, 'Yes, I'm sure you can find your own way downstairs,' and stalked off to her room. She had forgotten all about the garter belt she had left behind in the observatory, and trying to explain that away to Didi was going to be a mammoth task, she thought woefully. Didi had very strict ideas on how a lady should behave, and leaving one's garter belt in a man's bed was the equivalent of a lifelong commitment to the man, in her housekeeper's eyes. No wonder Didi had accepted Luc so readily...

Parisa leant against the bedroom door and took a few deep breaths, dragging the air into her lungs and holding it in an effort to restore her shattered nerves to some semblance of calm. Luc here in her home. The new Lord of the Manor. It was too incredible to believe. Slowly she crossed to the bed and sat down. She wasn't such a fool as to believe he had done it for her. Five days she had waited in London for him. Even if he could not leave Italy he could certainly have picked up a telephone and called her. He was here because of his mother. She could appreciate his dilemma, and in a way she felt partly responsible. After all, she had convinced Signora Di Maggi she was going to marry her son. Added to which, a cheque for thousands was in her bank account, and the knowledge that it was Luc's money was very hard to take. She had a sinking feeling that Luc would not agree to take the money back and restore the title to her. Why should he? The money was nothing to a man of his wealth, but his mother's health meant a lot to him. She wanted to refuse to go and visit the old lady, but her conscience wouldn't let her. She had taken his money, plus the ring, and felt some obligation...

She got to her feet and quickly dressed. She slipped on the blue velvet dress, not because she wanted to remind Luc of the first night in Italy, but because she needed to present a sophisticated image, she told herself. The ring, at least, she could give back and, picking up the small jewel box with the ring inside, she dashed downstairs, but headed for the kitchen. She had to speak to Didi and explain it was a mistake; she did not want the old lady hurt. Unfortunately she was foiled in her aim by Didi herself, who insisted there was no time to gossip and chased her into the drawing-room.

Parisa, her hostility exacerbated by Didi's blind acceptance of Luc, strode purposefully up to where he was standing, and without hesitation thrust the ring box into his hand.

'Yours, Mr Di Maggi. I'm sure you will have no difficulty in finding someone to wear it.'

'Parisa, *cara*, I never realized you were such a romantic.' And, to her horror, before she could stop him he had opened the box, removed the ring, and, dropping on one knee at her feet, gazed languidly up into her furious face. 'You will marry me, won't you, Parisa?' And, in front of a grinning Didi, he slipped the ring on her finger.

Her hoarse 'No!' went unheard as Didi exclaimed, 'What a one you are, Mr Luc.' While Parisa, her cheeks washed pink with a mixture of embarrassment and fury, found herself sitting down on the sofa, her small hands clenched in fury.

'I'll go and tell the chauffeur you're ready to leave,' was Didi's parting shot.

Parisa, her nerves screaming with tension, waited until the old lady had left. Then, turning ice-blue eyes on the man opposite, with a degree of iron control she had not thought herself capable of, she told him, 'I will wear this ring for one day only. I will go with you to visit your mother. But let me make this absolutely clear: I am doing it for two old ladies, not you... In return, in a few days you will place a repudiation in the newspaper, and you will never come to my home again. Agreed?' she demanded.

His arrogant head tilted back. 'If that is what you want, I agree. But let's discuss it over dinner.'

What she wanted was to step back in time a couple of months, she thought wryly, and never to have met Luc again. Unfortunately, that was impossible...

The Old Forge in Magum Down was a picturesque old English sixteenth-century forge that had been converted in the nineteen thirties into a small, privately owned hotel, and the restaurant was known for miles around for its excellent cuisine.

Parisa watched Luc break a piece of bread from the hot roll on his plate and pop it into his mouth. How was it that Luc could make the simplest act somehow sensual?

He caught her staring, his lips tilting at the corners in a brief, very masculine grin before saying, 'Eat your meal, Parisa, before it gets cold.'

'Mmm,' she mumbled, disconcerted by the quick stab of awareness that made her hand tremble slightly as she abruptly lowered her gaze to her plate and forked a tender piece of veal scallopine to her mouth. She wondered for the hundredth time why she was here, and what it was about Luc that meant that, even as she despised the high-handed way he had treated her, her body responded to his potent masculinity with a frightening intensity. 'More potatoes?' She offered him the dish in an attempt to get her mind back to the more mundane, but it didn't work.

'You remember my appetite... I'm flattered,' he said with a harsh laugh, accurately reading her mind. 'But do you recall everything, I wonder?' He leant back in his chair, eyeing her with cold disdain. 'Your body beneath mine, your hands clinging to me.' His low, deep-timbred drawl, the memories he awakened brought a flush of heat to her cheeks. 'No, you didn't care enough even to tell me where you lived.'

For a second she felt light-headed. Perhaps he *had* wanted to see her again, *did* care about her. But one glance at his set, angry expression, and she cursed herself for being a fool. She had waited in London for him to call, and he had never bothered. He wanted her now for his mother's sake.

'For heaven's sake keep your voice down,' she hissed, ignoring his provocative comment. 'This is a public restaurant.'

'So sorry, I wouldn't dream of embarrassing you.'

Liar... She wanted to scream her frustration to the heavens, but one glance at Luc's face, and she lowered her eyes. Why was he so angry with her? Surely it should be the other way around...?

Parisa lifted the fluted glass from the table and took a sip of the sparkling champagne, a gift from the proprietor and his wife. They had seen the announcement in *The Times*. She was a regular customer, and they knew her quite well. It had been a lovely gesture, but it only added to Parisa's feeling of guilt. She could not help feeling a complete fraud. The huge diamond on her finger and the rather large cheque she had paid into the bank that morning, all provided by the man sitting opposite her, did nothing to assuage her guilty feelings. Luc might have played a trick on her, but he had certainly paid very dearly for the privilege.

'Parisa, I did not bring you here to argue with you; quite the opposite. Will you marry me?'

Parisa choked on her wine and started to cough. She couldn't believe her ears. With her napkin held to her mouth, she raised watery eyes to her companion.

Luc, his expression remarkably bland, said smoothly, 'It was a straightforward question. I didn't expect you to choke on it.' His mouth relaxed, curling into a mocking smile as he studied her flushed face. 'But when you can speak I would like an answer.'

'No,' she spluttered, swallowing hard, her blue eyes wide as saucers in a face now pale with shock. Twice today he had asked her to marry him, and yet if he had asked her two months ago she would have jumped at the chance. But now she was much wiser...

'Impulsive as ever, Parisa. You haven't considered the prospect at all.' He laughed, a hint of devilment lurking in his eyes, as he reached across the table and wiped a stray tear from her cheek. 'Think about it. All your frustrating...problems solved at one go. I am a very wealthy, legitimate businessman, not—as you seemed to think—a crook. You spend two weeks as my wife, visit my mother, and a large amount of cash will be deposited in your bank account.'

The sheer arrogance, the conceit. And what did he mean, 'frustrating'...? Deposit money... As if she would consider for one minute...

'But you are a liar. You quite happily let me think you were a villain, a member of the Mafia. I was a huge joke to you, nothing more,' she said bitterly. 'It was only by chance I read in a Sunday newspaper you were a businessman and not a criminal.' That still rankled every time she thought of it. 'You had Luigi Reno charged with fraud, but you were not above using his filthy photographs to trick me. In fact you are just as much a blackmailer as he was.'

'But it didn't stop you going to bed with me, *cara*,' he reminded her silkily. 'Or enjoying it.'

'I don't need you to remind me what a fool I was,' she snapped, her eyes spitting fury.

'You don't know what you need,' she thought she heard him murmur, before he returned his attention to the food in front of him.

Her mouth curved with a hint of bitterness. How like him to drop a bombshell and then ignore her. Over two months had passed since she had spent the night in his arms, and now he had the nerve... To hide her shock and anger she picked up her glass of champagne and gulped it down.

'More wine?' Luc said urbanely, and refilled her glass. 'Finish your meal and think about it, Parisa.' And for the next few minutes silence reigned, as Luc cleared his plate with obvious relish, then added, 'Didi was right about this place. The food is superb.'

'Yes,' Parisa responded mechanically, eating without even tasting the delicious food, her mind in too much of a turmoil to concentrate on the meal.

'Good. I have a special licence for Thursday. We will marry at eleven and visit *Mamma* before she goes into Theatre.'

'No, I meant yes, the food is great,' she spluttered. She was too stunned by the events of the last few hours to think straight, and it did not help at all to realise Luc was laughing at her.

'Are you sure you have given my proposal careful consideration, Parisa? Earlier this evening you were telling me about your rather reckless ancestors, and decrying the fact none of them had any business sense. Yet here you are turning down an excellent proposition without a second thought.'

His black eyes held hers, a hint of challenge in their depths, and a wave of something very like fear washed over her. Until that moment she had almost succeeded in convincing herself that nothing Luc did could threaten her, but now she was not so sure.

'You must have inherited the reckless genes apparent in most of your ancestors,' Luc offered with open mockery.

'I have not...' she snapped back, her brief fear forgotten by his taunt. 'I...' and she stopped. He was right; she had not given her reply any thought. Maybe it was time she got her wandering mind under control and behaved sensibly. Since the moment she had seen Luc today, she had only reacted to him, not thought for herself. It was not like her to rush into anything. She prided herself on her calm logic, didn't she? 'What exactly do you mean by "proposition"?' she asked warily, studying his handsome face, the candle in the centre of the table casting flickering shadows over his rugged features.

'It is quite straightforward. As I told you, *Mamma* is in hospital. On Thursday she is scheduled for surgery. I want my mother to see me married before she goes under the surgeon's knife, and you, I believe, want an adequate income to restore your family home. I know you have the money I paid for the title, but that won't go far, and you will very quickly be back in the same position as you were before—needing money. If you agree to marry me, I will settle an allowance on you for life, and in addition I will spend whatever is necessary to completely refurbish and repair your home immediately. In return, all I need from you is your presence as my wife in London on Thursday and for about two weeks at most. A straightforward business deal. You will only have to work, or act...two weeks for it.'

Her glance trailed freely over his head and shoulders as he spoke. He looked stunningly attractive, if casually dressed. The white high-necked cashmere sweater, with his leather jacket draped loosely over his broad shoulders, somehow made him seem more of a foreigner to Parisa, and very Latin. She glanced around. Every other man in the restaurant wore a tie, and yet Luc still managed to look the most elegant. She had listened to his proposition and knew he did not really want her as his wife, and she would be a fool to think otherwise. But in the circumstances, wasn't that a plus factor in the deal? she argued with herself.

'A fortnight of my life for a fortune, that's all...?' she prompted with a trace of sarcasm, her blue eyes clashing with enigmatic black ones, as bravely she held his gaze.

'Yes, that is all. According to Didi, you have almost three weeks of the Easter vacation left; our little arrangement will not affect your work. It will be completed in time for you to return to school for the summer term. It couldn't be more convenient. Think, Parisa—all your money problems solved, Didi and Joe assured of a happy retirement, and yourself free of the constant worry of trying to maintain the manor house. I am an extremely wealthy man and I am prepared to pay a lot for my *mamma's* peace of mind.'

The way he spoke, cool and business-like, did much to persuade her he actually meant what he was saying. 'No strings attached?' she queried. He was right; she would never get a better offer to put her house in order, both literally and metaphorically speaking. She rubbed her damp palms surreptitiously on the smooth velvet of her skirt, under the table. Finally she would be able to pay Didi and Joe a pension.

'None at all. You have my word. We get married in the register office on Thursday. We stay in my hotel suite and visit the hospital daily, say ten days or so, which is when the consultant believes my mother will be fit enough to return to Italy. But, whatever happens, you can return to Hardcourt Manor in time to go back to work.'

'Won't your mother find it odd, my vanishing after such a short time?' she asked, completely missing the flash of triumph in Luc's dark eyes at her unconscious acceptance.

'Not in the least. We'll tell her about the refurbishment of the manor, and obviously, as the mistress, you will be needed to oversee everything. I will be coming to England much more frequently now I own a company here. So there is no reason for Mother to suspect anything wrong between you and I.'

'You appear to have thought of everything,' Parisa said musingly, and drank some more champagne. 'But eventually your mother is bound to want to see me.'

'The prognosis for my mother is not great, even with the operation. A year or two at most. Afterwards, a quick divorce for you and I.'

Compassion softened Parisa's blue eyes. 'I'm sorry...I didn't realise her condition was so bad.'

'Why should you? She is little more than a stranger to you. But if you agree, it is in your power to make the

rest of her life much happier.' Parisa knew he was telling
the truth. The sincerity in his black eyes was unmistakable as he held her wary gaze. 'Say yes...'

'Why me?' she murmured softly. Luc knew lots of
women, any one of whom would jump at the chance of
being his wife, without it costing him a fraction of what
he seemed to be prepared to pay her. Once again he
seemed to read her mind.

'You forget my mother already believes you and I are
engaged. Personally I have no more desire to get married
than you have, and, flattering though it is that you imagine I can marry any woman at will, Parisa, consider:
if I produce a total stranger tomorrow as my prospective
bride it is hardly likely to reassure my mother,' he commented cynically.

Determined to decide with her head, logically, Parisa
picked up her glass and drained it, carefully replacing it
on the table. What he said made a lot of sense. Except
it was Luc Di Maggi saying it... No, it was impossible.
Wasn't it?

'You can't lose, Parisa. I noticed everyone around here
uses your title. What are you going to tell them, that
you are no longer a Lady? That title is reserved for the
woman I marry.'

'That is no argument. I couldn't care less about the
title—I wouldn't have sold it if I did,' she replied bluntly.
But the odd pain in the region of her heart at the thought
of Luc married to someone else she swiftly dismissed as
indigestion.

She tilted her head to one side, her silver-gilt hair
falling in a swathe over her shoulder; she had left it loose
tonight. Not because Luc preferred it that way... She
had simply been in a hurry. She rested her elbow on the
table and twisted a strand of pale hair around her finger,
while openly studying Luc. She could read nothing from
his rugged, if somewhat gaunt features; a bit tired,
maybe, but his cool dark eyes seemed honest enough as

they met hers. Dared she trust him, and did it matter for only two weeks...?

'Yes, all right. I agree; it's a deal.' And, stretching out her slender hand, 'Shake on it.'

Luc caught her hand in his much larger one and said very gravely, 'A deal, Parisa.' And then to her astonishment he raised her hand to his lips and kissed the back of it, his mouth warm on her soft flesh. 'Thank you.'

She couldn't respond. Instead, she was trying to rub the tingling feeling from the back of her hand, under the cover of the table, and wondering if she had just made the biggest mistake of her life.

Luc didn't give her time to change her mind, as over dessert and coffee he talked non-stop. Parisa wasn't very sure what about, and when they finally stood up to leave she was beginning to wonder if she had imagined agreeing to marry him.

She walked out of the restaurant in a daze, but was brought back to the present by the sound of Luc crying out.

'Ouch!' She swung around, and saw him sway, then straighten. Parisa couldn't help it: she burst out laughing. He had his eyes closed and was dramatically holding a hand to his head.

'This is a very old establishment, and the oak beams and low ceilings part of its charm. You should be more careful. It does say in very large letters over the dining room door: "Mind your Head".'

His 'Ha, ha...' ended in a groan.

'Are you OK?' Parisa walked back to Luc and placed a hand on his arm. 'You hurt yourself?' He looked very pale. At that moment the chauffeur walked out of the adjoining bar.

'No, I'm fine.' And Luc, straightening his broad shoulders, took her arm and led her out to the car.

Seated in the back seat of the limousine, she moved close to the window, putting as much space between herself and Luc as humanly possible.

'You have nothing to fear, Parisa...' He cast her a sidelong glance, one brow arched sardonically. 'I have no burning desire to leap on you, or, at present, the energy. Our marriage will be strictly business.'

'I wouldn't agree otherwise,' she replied firmly, but some imp of mischief deep down inside her queried the truth of her comment.

CHAPTER EIGHT

THE car stopped outside the oak double doors of her home. Parisa cast a sidelong glance at Luc. His head was back against the seat and his eyes were closed. The dim light of the car cast a greyish tinge over his taut features. For a moment she wondered if the knock on the head had hurt him more than he wanted to admit. His long lashes fluttered on his cheeks and his eyes opened. For a second they did not seem to focus, but with a grunt he straightened up in the seat.

His dark head bent towards her as he reached across to open the car door. 'You will excuse me if I don't get out, but the chauffeur will see you to the door, and pick you up again in the morning around ten. I will meet you at the hospital and together we can tell *Mamma* the good news.'

'Yes—yes, fine,' she stuttered, the husky male scent of him, his nearness making her uneasy!

'Parisa.' He caught her hand as she swung her long legs out of the car. 'No second thoughts. I expect to see you in the morning. Our deal stands...'

'Yes, OK.'

There was something distant about him, and he seemed to be slurring his words. Parisa slid out of the car, and looked back.

'Get in the house,' he commanded curtly.

Turning, she walked up the steps and let herself in the front door. She locked the heavy door behind her, and tiredly walked across the hall to the stairs, the portraits of her ancestors smiling down at her. She had the oddest feeling that they were laughing at her. She shook her head to dispel the fanciful notion and wearily climbed the grand staircase.

She stopped at the antiquated bathroom next door to her bedroom, and, stripping off her clothes, had a quick wash, and, taking her old towelling robe from the back of the door, gratefully made her way to the bedroom. Shrugging out of her robe, she climbed into the welcoming softness of the huge old bed. She didn't want to think, just sleep.

But it was not so easy. Had she really agreed to marry Luc on Thursday? It made sense financially, she knew, but what about emotionally? Could she live with the man even for two weeks without resurrecting all the hurt and pain she had already suffered at his hands? Did she have the strength of will, or even the acting ability to play the part he wanted from her? A million questions swirled around her tired mind, and she wasn't capable of answering them.

Perhaps, she thought, turning restlessly on the bed, it was all a joke. Tomorrow Luc would ring and tell her it was all off. She half hoped he would. He had told her to use her head, have a bit of business sense, and she could see the advantages of his offer very clearly. True, she did feel sorry for his mother, and felt some slight obligation as she had led the lady to believe she was engaged to her son. Didi as well would be delighted at the thought of Parisa marrying Luc. But basically, what did it make her; Parisa Hardcourt-Belmont, going through a marriage ceremony mainly for money... A harsh, humourless laugh escaped her. Mercenary! But then, was that so strange? In the history of her family there had been plenty of arranged marriages, and no doubt some strictly for money. Why should she balk at the thought?

Love was for fools; she had learnt that lesson the hard way. Luc Di Maggi had taught her. She remembered when he had first broached the subject of her going to Italy with him, and he had said he would never marry, but he didn't mind getting engaged to keep his mother happy. Maybe that was Parisa's guarantee. He was a ruthless, dynamic businessman, who had, from the humble beginnings of a bakery, built a vast empire. He took what he wanted without a thought for other people. How many people had he used and cast aside along the way, herself included? she wondered.

She might despise the man. The five days she had waited in London for him to get in touch with her had been the most painful period she had ever endured. She had deluded herself into believing Luc must love her simply because she loved him. Then, the final day, she had seen the newspaper article, and realised Luc had lied to her, that the man she had thought she was in love with, the man she had even been prepared to accept was a criminal at the cost of her own conscience, was a stranger to her. Parisa had given herself to a man who had simply been playing a joke on her as some petty revenge for a supposed insult of years ago. When she had realised the extent of her naïveté, she had vowed that no man would get the chance to make a fool of her again.

Could she be as hard and cynical as Luc was? Yes . . . She would take his money, she told herself with bitter certainty. Why not? Who more appropriate? After all, he had bought the title, and the thought really rankled. She grumbled about the old building, but in reality she loved her home and could not imagine living anywhere else. Her childhood memories of running wild around the five acres of parkland . . . playing hide-and-seek with her father in the many rooms . . . sliding down the banister . . . She cherished her memories, but from now on, for the rest of her life, she would have to live with the ever present knowledge that Luc was the Lord of the Manor.

She deserved the money, she told herself, and there was no denying it would be much easier for her personally. Legally, as Luc's wife, if only in name and for a short duration, her position would remain the same and there would be no need for her to reveal to friends and acquaintances that she had actually sold the title.

Cowardly, perhaps, but she had not relished the thought of exposing her monetary problems to all and sundry. But the deciding factor was that it would enable her to pay Didi and Joe a decent pension for the rest of their lives. But it was still a long time before she finally slept, and when she did her dreams were full of a tall tanned man, black eyes gleaming with devilish humour, laughing down at her.

Parisa awakened the next morning and almost convinced herself the previous day had been a dream or, more likely, a nightmare. Luc had stormed back into her life, announcing to the world at large that she was his fiancée. She had no illusions about him caring for her... He had made it brutally obvious yesterday afternoon, with his cutting remark about the night he had made love to her. So why was she being stupid enough to go along with his crazy plan to get married, even if it was only for a couple of weeks? she asked herself. Deceiving Didi! Wearing his ring! She had no answer. Well, none she was prepared to admit to.

She did not love him... Her trip to Italy had been stupid, even though her reason for going had been compelling at the time. But a fortnight in London, a strictly platonic relationship, for a fortune... Surely it was common sense to accept...?

She groaned. Her head was pounding, and Didi's hearty 'Good morning' as she walked into the room, a cup of coffee in her hand, did not help.

'You'd better get up, Miss Parisa. There is a man downstairs waiting for you to show him the house!'

'What? Who?' she murmured, hauling herself up the bed and tucking the sheet around under her arms. She took the proffered cup of coffee and downed it in one go. She had drunk far too much champagne last night and she wasn't used to it.

'A Mr Smythe; he's an architect. Mr Luc sent him to decide what needs doing and how. Isn't it marvellous?'

'Yes, great.' Parisa groaned as the enormity of what she had agreed to hit her. Luc had certainly wasted no time, she thought angrily. Obviously he was taking no chances on her changing her mind. She barely had time to wash and slip on her leather suit before the limousine arrived to take her to the hospital.

Parisa stepped out of the car outside the main entrance to the hospital, and before she had time to sling her shoulder-bag over her shoulder Luc was at her elbow.

'Good, you've arrived. Mother will be pleased.' And, without so much as a 'Good morning', he was ushering her into the hospital.

'Hello to you, too,' she said sarcastically, glancing sideways at his handsome face. He still looked rather pale and she wondered if it was solely because of his concern for his mother. Or perhaps it was the thought of getting married, even briefly? He was not the marrying type, as he had told her more than once. This morning he was wearing a smart two-piece navy suit, with a high-necked Cossack-style blue silk shirt and no tie. It should have looked affected, she thought wryly, but on Luc it looked stunning.

They stepped into the lift with two white-coated girls, who couldn't take their eyes off Luc. Parisa smiled grimly. He was that sort of man: he attracted females like bees to honey.

Then Luc was leading her into the private room on the second floor, and all her attention was captured by the lady lying in the bed. Her eyes widened with shock. Signora Di Maggi looked nothing like the strapping woman she had met two months ago. How could someone change so much in so short a time? she wondered, forcing herself to smile as she crossed to the bedside.

'Hello, Signora Di Maggi. What have you been doing?' And, bending down, she pressed her lips to the lined cheek, the skin like dry parchment beneath her lips.

The old lady smiled, her dark eyes so like her son's, but full of moisture. 'Parisa. It is lovely you are here, and to be married. I am so happy...'

Luc stood at the opposite side of the bed, his whole attention centred on the occupant, a smile of such warmth and love on his face that Parisa had to stifle a gasp of amazement. 'You must not talk too much, *Mamma*, and no excitement. Doctor's orders.' And, leaning over the bed, he kissed the top of her white head, while gathering her slender hands in his massive ones. He sat on the side of the bed, and for a few moments mother and son simply looked at each other.

Parisa felt like an intruder, and silently she sat down on the chair beside the bed, staring at her hands entwined on her lap. She felt a swift stab of guilt as the huge ring on her finger glittered with a brilliant light. Before, when she had thought it was simple costume jewellery, it had not bothered her, but now she was constantly aware of it. She had no doubt that what Luc had said was true. It was a rare and costly diamond. She must have been blind not to notice the true value. If she had been thinking logically at the time of the party, she would have realised that Luc might produce a fake fiancée to fool his family, but he would never have insulted their intelligence by producing a fake ring. But what of a fake marriage? It wasn't right, what she and Luc were doing to his mother. She gnawed at her bottom lip, frowning. The old lady deserved the truth.

Half an hour later when they got up to leave, Parisa did not need a doctor to tell her the visit had done Signora Di Maggi good. She was smiling and obviously content.

Luc walked around the bed and flung a casual arm around Parisa's shoulder. She tensed, but did not pull away, in deference to the old lady's feelings. And when, with an aside to his mother, Luc turned Parisa into his arms, bent his dark head, his mouth covering hers in a deep, gentle kiss, she almost imagined he meant it, her body melting against his as his mastery of her senses overcame her logical mind. It was a flushed and very worried girl who finally walked out of the hospital, with Luc retaining a firm grip on her hand.

He stopped beside the waiting car, and, opening the rear door, he finally let go of her hand. 'Sorry I can't accompany you, but the chauffeur will see you safely home. I will send the car for you on Thursday morning, but I'll call you before then with the details.'

'Luc, I'm not sure...' The deep unease she felt about their deal had increased a hundredfold. How much her agreement had had to do with the amount of champagne she had drunk the previous evening she was beginning to question, but Luc never gave her a chance. She was bundled into the car before she could finish her sentence.

'It's too late to change your mind, Parisa.'

Luc, resplendent in an immaculate light grey silk suit and white shirt, and a silk tie in conservative tones of grey and maroon, looked exactly what he was: a mature, sophisticated man of the world.

Parisa, on the other hand, felt like a naïve teenager in comparison. It was stupid, she knew. It made good business sense. She should not be intimidated; after all, it was only a civil ceremony, easily cast aside. So why were her legs trembling?

Dressed in a pale cream suit, a touch of a peach camisole peeping between the lapels of the fitted jacket, the skirt short and straight, ending on her knees, her feet encased in matching high-heeled pumps, and her hands clasping a small clutch-bag with an exquisite posy of tiny peach rosebuds and baby breath pinned to the front, Parisa listened to the registrar, but didn't take anything in. It was only when Didi gave her elbow a nudge that she surfaced from her daze long enough to say, 'I do.' She looked with sightless eyes at the gold band Luc slid on her finger. But when he turned and gathered her into his arms, all her senses went on red alert.

'My wife,' he murmured just before his lips covered hers in a brief, hard kiss.

'You look beautiful, Miss Parisa,' Didi remarked as they stood in the powder-room at the Ritz, having just finished a celebratory wedding breakfast. 'You will be happy, child, trust your old nanny. I had a long talk to Luc the other day, before you arrived, and he does love you very much. He gave me back the red garter belt you had left in Italy.' The old eyes twinkled, as Parisa blushed scarlet. 'Now, don't you worry none. There are plenty of young women jumped the gun a bit, I understand.' She chuckled. 'I knew over the past months you had been pining for someone, and once I met Luc I knew why. But now everything will be perfect.'

No wonder Didi had been so keen to see her married, Parisa thought; she probably imagined Parisa was already pregnant. Luc had taken charge. He had called the house yesterday, spoken briefly to Parisa, but longer to Didi. Parisa had been rushed into Brighton by Didi, and suitable outfits purchased.

Parisa sighed inwardly. How could she disillusion the old lady? Didi and her husband, Joe, had been the witnesses at the wedding ceremony, the only guests. In fact they had been instrumental in her decision to accept Luc's proposal. The couple had looked after her all her life, and they were entitled to some monetary security in their old age. It had worried her for ages how she was going to provide for them. Now, the problem was solved. If nothing else good came out of the next two weeks, the peace of mind that knowing the two people she cared for most in the world were looked after was more than enough. She left the powder-room arm in arm with Didi.

'Parisa.' Luc's dark gaze lingered on her lovely face as he approached her; his large hands curved possess-ively around her shoulder. 'I think everything went off very well, don't you, *cara*?'

She tilted her head to look up at him, and the gleam of mocking triumph in his black eyes sent a shiver down her spine. 'Yes,' she said curtly, and, following the older couple out of the hotel to the waiting taxi and limousine, she chewed her lip nervously. Just what had that look meant?

It was with a sigh of relief that she finally waved goodbye to the taxi carrying Didi and Joe back to Hardcourt Manor and turned towards the chauffeured limousine waiting at the kerb. Luc took her arm and helped her into the car, sliding his large body in beside her.

'Alone at last,' he drawled and, catching her left hand in his, he twirled the plain gold ring on her finger. 'I never thought I would ever put a gold ring on any woman's finger.' His hard mouth curved in a cynical smile. 'Diamonds, maybe, but this...' And in a totally unexpected gesture he lifted her hand to his mouth and kissed the wedding band.

Her heart gave a curious lurch, her blue eyes clashed with black, and the glittering intensity of his gaze shot sparks of sensual awareness careering through her body. She pulled her hand free, and tore her eyes from his. She opened her handbag and withdrew the engagement ring she had thought a fake, and put it on her finger. Somehow the sight of the huge diamond reminded her of the true reason for this marriage and she was not going to forget it. Show!

'Have I told you yet how beautiful you look? The perfect bride, with just the right amount of innocent reluctance.' He moved his long legs, his thigh brushing hers apparently unconsciously. 'I am a fortunate man to have won such a perfect wife,' Luc opined, but the underlying anger in his tone was not lost on Parisa. Luc had never wanted to marry...

Your business partner,' she said pointedly and put a foot of space between them, before adding, 'Isn't it time we were at the hospital?' She held the posy of roses in front of her like a shield. 'I think your mother will like these.' She was determined to keep her distance from Luc. Cool, calm and collected for two weeks, she vowed over and over in her head.

It was a short drive across London to the hospital, and, when they finally reached Signora De Maggi's private room, to Parisa's eyes his mother looked even frailer than two days ago. She gently handed the old woman the posy and thought it was almost worth marrying Luc just to see the happiness—and yes, relief—reflected in her tired dark eyes.

'I'm so happy for you both.' Her eyes filled with tears. 'Now I know Luc has someone, I can rest easy.'

'Don't say that, *Mamma*,' Luc admonished huskily. 'You will be fine, and then we will have a grand party in Italy,' he joked, and spent the next few minutes making her laugh.

But when the nurse came and ordered them to leave, as Signora Di Maggi was to be prepared for surgery, the smile was wiped from Luc's face in a second.

The waiting-room was a miserable place, the walls a stark white, the furniture comfortable armchairs and a low table, and Parisa could almost feel sorry for Luc. He sat down and she sat opposite him.

He glanced across at her, his eyes as cold as the arctic waste. He slid a large hand into his breast pocket and withdrew a long envelope, throwing it on the table between them. 'You'd better read that and then sign it. I think you will find it is all in order.'

She shot a surprised glance at his rugged face. 'Now?' His mother was going into Theatre, for God's sake! And her sympathy for the man vanished.

' "Business partners" was the term you used, Parisa. That is the agreement; read it and sign.'

She picked up the papers and began to read. A gasp escaped her at the size of the allowance mentioned. He had certainly been very generous, so why wasn't she ecstatic at the thought? Instead, all she felt was self-disgust. She had sunk to his level where everything had a price, and without really taking everything in. She asked stiltedly, 'Have you a pen I can borrow?'

Luc handed her an elegant gold pen, and, without a word being spoken, she signed the document and passed it back to him. Being hard and cynical was not going to be as easy as she had first thought...

They spent all afternoon and into the evening hardly exchanging a word, a nurse bringing the occasional cup of coffee the only diversion, until at eight o'clock the doctor arrived. The operation had been a success.

Luc grasped her hand in his as the nurse led them to the intensive care unit. His mother was lying, apparently asleep, with various tubes attached to her, but her colour did look slightly better.

'She'll be fine, Luc,' Parisa murmured.

'Yes, I think she will now...' he sighed. 'Thank you, Parisa.' And he let go of her hand.

After another ride across London, the driver dropped them off at the entrance to the hotel. As Luc ushered her inside she had a brief impression of a comfortable, elegant entrance foyer, traditional in appearance with thick carpeting and velvet drapes.

Parisa stood to one side as Luc talked briefly to the receptionist and a key changed hands, then Luc turned back to her. 'The chauffeur delivered your luggage earlier. Would you like to eat dinner down here in the restaurant or in our suite?'

'I'm not really hungry,' she said without thinking, but wished she hadn't as Luc agreed and, taking her arm, led her to the lift.

They rode up to the top floor in silence. The doors slid open and Luc ushered Parisa out across a wide hall, turned the key in the lock of the door and, with a hand on her back, urged her inside. The door opened straight on to a large square sitting-room. A deep pile carpet covered the floor. An Adam-style fireplace, the coals aglow, was the focal point of one wall. Parisa guessed it was a gas effect, but it was welcoming all the same. Two comfortable settees with a low coffee-table between them were the room's main furniture, along with a television, a couple of lamp tables and a small writing-desk with a telephone on the top.

'The bedrooms are through there.' Luc gestured to a small hall. 'You can check later. Right now I need a shower and a drink. Fix me a whisky and soda, please, and order a plate of... oh, sandwiches, whatever you fancy.' And, not waiting for her response, he disappeared down the hall.

Parisa heaved a sigh of relief. He had said 'bedrooms', plural; she had nothing to fear. In fact it should not be too hard to keep out of Luc's way over the next fortnight, apart from the hospital visits. Crossing to the complimentary bar, she filled two crystal tumblers with one generous and one smaller measure of whisky, adding ice and soda.

Taking the weaker of the two, she wandered back to the middle of the room and sank down on the comfortable sofa, kicking her shoes off and undoing the buttons of her jacket to reveal the peach silk camisole beneath. Tilting her head back, she took a reviving swallow of the amber liquid. Then, placing the glass on the table, she picked up the telephone, and quickly ordered sandwiches and coffee.

Retrieving her glass, she took another sip of the spirit, and looked around the subdued elegance of the room. It would be very easy to get used to this lifestyle, she thought musingly, but then, once she had got through the next couple of weeks, she would be able to afford this lifestyle. Somehow the thought did not make her as happy as she had hoped.

Parisa had never coveted wealth. She enjoyed her work, and as long as she could make ends meet she was quite happy. So what had happened to her usual easy-going nature to make her agree to Luc's proposition? Bitterness, greed: unenviable emotions, her innate honesty forced her to acknowledge, but it was too late; she had agreed. She jerked upright, spilling a little of her drink, as Luc's voice broke into her musing.

'Mine, I presume?' He was standing in front of her, his huge body stooped to pick up the drink she had prepared for him, and the sheer size and strength of him, along with his state of undress, hit her like a punch in the solar plexus.

He was wearing a white towelling robe, belted loosely at the waist and ending halfway down his muscular thighs. His golden-tanned skin and mat of black body hair was exposed between the low lapels of the garment. Suddenly she was made aware of just what kind of intimacy she had invited by agreeing to a marriage of convenience, and she swallowed nervously, her hand tightening on her glass. God, if she wasn't careful she was going to end up an alky before long, she thought, draining her drink. Luc had an alarming ability to set every nerve in her body into a jangling mass of hyper-activity. Luckily a knock on the door heralded the arrival of the waiter with the supper.

Parisa barely touched the food; she had hardly eaten anything all day, in fact, and she felt light-headed. Deliberately she stood up, tensing as Luc also rose from the sofa opposite.

'I'm tired; it's been a long day. I think I'll go to bed now,' she managed to say firmly, but she could not meet his dark, watchful eyes. She crossed the room in her stockinged feet. Feeling small and very vulnerable, she scuttled along the hall without looking back and entered the first door. Her eyes widened in puzzlement. It wasn't a bedroom, but more like an office, with computer, fax

and telephone on a huge desk. Swinging around, she
walked out and tried the next door along.

It was a large room with a king-sized bed in the centre,
four-posted and elegantly draped in swish gold and blue
velvet. Her suitcase was standing by an ornate antique
dressing-table. She heaved a sigh of relief; this must be
her room.

She opened her suitcase and grimaced at the floaty
white wisp of silk and lace lying on the top, a note attached. A present from Didi. She rummaged deeper, and
to her disgust found her sensible nightshirt was nowhere
to be found. Frowning, she quickly hung her few clothes
in the capacious wardrobe, and, reluctantly picking up
the froth of white and her toilet things, she walked into
the adjoining bathroom. In minutes she had a shower.
Drying herself quickly with a thick, fluffy towel, she
slipped the offending nightdress over her head.

A brief glance in the mirror did nothing to reassure
her. Tiny plaited spaghetti straps held a bodice of
gossamer lace that barely covered her breasts; the skirt
was a swirl of transparent silk. Poor Didi; she was such
a romantic. Shrugging fatalistically—no one was going
to see it—Parisa returned to the bedroom, and stopped
dead...

She stood transfixed, her mouth hanging open.
Sprawled across the huge bed, wearing only a tiny pair
of white briefs, was Luc. His black eyes glittered fiercely
as he turned his head to study her with blatant
thoroughness that made her whole body blush.

'Very sexy and quite bridal,' he taunted mockingly.

'What the hell do you think you're doing? This is my
room,' she cried, swallowing hard on the ball of fear
that lodged in her throat. Her eyes met his and she
flinched at the furious intent she saw in them.

CHAPTER NINE

'*OUR* bedroom, Parisa.' Luc's mocking voice echoed in the silence. He swung his long legs off the bed and sauntered across the room, his intention obvious.

Parisa stayed frozen to the spot. She lowered her eyes on a level with his chest and folded her arms across her body in an instinctive gesture of defence, her anger evaporating as fear paralysed her.

'Forget it, Luc,' Parisa warned him, taking a cautious step back. 'You said *bedrooms*, plural... You said no strings...' she insisted, tearing her eyes away from the golden skin and glistening black body hair. Memories rose up to taunt her, of herself once welcoming his magnificent body. She stifled a groan, reluctantly raising her eyes to his, but the predatory sensual glitter in his gaze made her flesh prickle in a totally unwanted response.

'A business deal, two weeks... for your mother...' She was babbling. 'You lied.'

'No, I didn't lie. There are two bedrooms, one I use as an office. I lease this suite on a permanent basis. As for the rest, you agreed to be my wife for a limited time, with everything that entails, Parisa,' he taunted, stopping only inches away from her.

She unfolded her arms to push him away, but she was caught off guard by the speed with which he moved, hauling her against the hard heat of his tall, powerful body. 'No, no...' she pleaded, shaking her head, her silver-blonde hair flowing around her shoulders, as she

147

tried to twist away, but he held her firm, moulding her to his almost naked form.

'Don't be a fool, Parisa. Did you really expect me to part with a fortune for nothing? As it is, you are probably the most expensive lady I have ever possessed.' Her head jerked back as with one hand he twisted a swathe of hair around his wrist. 'And I intend to get my money's worth,' he declared with implacable resolution.

Possess her? Never! But as her mind screamed *no* she went rigid, shrinking from the terrible cynical determination in his black eyes. He towered over her, the domineering strength of the man implicit in every line of his huge frame.

'Luc...you can't,' she implored. 'Our deal didn't include...sex.' She forced the word out through trembling lips. Maybe if she didn't struggle, if she reasoned with him, she thought, desperately aware of the leashed tension in his taut, muscular body.

'Sex was never mentioned, my sweet Parisa. If you remember, you were too much of a lady to spell it out. Which suited me just fine.' He smiled derisively, his narrowed gaze blazing with triumph and a raw sensual message that petrified her.

What he said made a terrible kind of sense. He was right, and the knowledge destroyed what little confidence she had left. His dark head bent and he brought his mouth down savagely upon hers, forcing her lips to part to the thrusting, shockingly sensual invasion of his tongue.

Heat coursed through her in wave after wave, rocking her with the force of his angry passion. She whimpered low in her throat as he broke the kiss, freeing her swollen mouth while his hand slid lower down her back, urging her hips into intimate contact with the fierce potency of his arousal.

'Feel what you do to me, wife, and know that I am going to sate myself in your beautiful, heartless body,' he said with bitter ferocity. 'So I can walk away with no regret.'

She felt sick, her stomach churning with nausea. He hated her; she could see it in his eyes, feel it in the savage pull on her hair, but she couldn't understand why. She had sensed the underlying anger in him ever since he had turned up at her home, but had closed her mind to it. Her own bitterness had been more than enough for her to control. Now she wished she had queried his hidden rage.

'Let me free, Luc,' she gasped, as his lips touched her bare shoulder. She struck out wildly at his head, but he let go of her hair and captured her wrists, pinioning them behind her with one hand. 'You can't do this,' she cried, but there was no mercy in his eyes as they surveyed her pale, beautiful face, as he forced her back against his arm before, with his free hand, he deliberately slipped the straps of her nightgown down her arms, revealing her naked breasts to his hungry gaze.

'You can't force me to make lo...' But his head bent once more, his mouth moving with deliberate sensuality down the long line of her throat, and lower, to the soft curve of her full breasts. He nibbled and licked like some great jungle cat, the touch of his tongue on the sensitive flesh of her breast inducing a helpless languor in her heated body.

She moaned, 'No,' as his strong hand cupped her breast, his fingers teasing the tight nipple with devastating effect, while his lips covered the other one, drawing the hard nub into the hot dark warmth of his mouth.

Her breath stopped in her throat, as an ache of longing, so basic, so primitive swept through her. She closed her eyes as she helplessly acknowledged that she ached for the fulfilment only Luc could provide. She hated her own wanton response, and with her last tiny thread of control she cried, 'No, I don't want this.'

'Now who is the liar, Parisa? I don't need to force you. You're aching for it, my passionate little cat,' Luc muttered hoarsely, lifting his head to stare into her flushed face.

She opened her eyes, and met the glittering black cynical gaze of her tormentor. 'I should never have trusted you. I hate you,' she breathed hoarsely.

'You know what they say about love and hate, *cara*.' His arm tightened around her back and effortlessly he swept her off her feet and crossed to the huge bed, his mouth slowly descending towards hers. 'Either emotion will do for me as long as this luscious body of yours responds so fiercely.' He murmured the words as his lips slid across her brow, and down her cheek. Parisa felt the mattress beneath her as his sensuous lips once more found hers.

'I don't...' she cried, but the cry was lost beneath the pressure of his mouth, as he kissed her with a hot, ruthless passion. His huge body pinned her to the bed; she could feel the heavy pounding of his heart against her breast. The brush of his hand through the tangled mass of her hair was oddly soothing as his lips gentled on hers. She tried to ease her hands between them to push him away, but when her fingers felt the rock-hard muscle of his chest all her resistance vanished. Instead, her hands moved of their own volition, her fingers tracing the hard male nipples, curling in the soft masculine body hair in secret delight.

'That's better, Parisa. Touch me. You want to, you know you do.' He breathed the husky encouragement against the tender skin of her throat, while his hand stroked expertly down over her breast, the indentation of her waist. Moving to one side, he slid the nightgown down her legs and flung it to the floor, at the same time removing his briefs.

She could have escaped; for a second she was free, but her mind had stopped functioning. Her blue eyes widened on his magnificent nude torso. She was drowning in a sea of sensations and memories that paled into insignificance when presented with the reality of the man. Her fingers, with a life of their own, reached out and stroked lower over his stomach, exploring the miracle of his essential maleness.

Luc groaned, and, grasping her straying hand, placed it on his shoulder before moving over her and cupping her face in the palms of his hands. For a moment, his black eyes burnt into hers.

'You want this, Parisa; tell me,' he demanded throatily.

She closed her eyes, trying to blot out the image of him, but his hard-muscled body moved seductively against her. Her hand on his shoulder slid down his chest, her other arm going around him, tracing the muscle and sinew of his broad back with achingly familiar delight.

'Yes,' she moaned, her surrender against his mouth as their lips met again.

Luc, like a man possessed, kissed her mouth, her eyes, the gentle curve of her chin. His teeth bit lightly over the madly beating pulse in her throat.

Desire, passion, need: they drank the explosive cocktail as they drank of each other. Luc's mouth and hands caressed and stroked, suckled and probed every intimate part of her, until Parisa was a mindless, molten entity, wanting nothing but to lose herself in the miracle of his possession. She traced her hands down his sides and around his firm buttocks, the potent force of his masculine arousal a hard, exciting pressure against her thigh.

'God, but I want you,' Luc groaned, and with one knee he parted her shapely legs, his long fingers finding and stroking the damp, sensitive flesh at the very centre of her femininity with slow, sensual pleasure. Only his laboured breathing and the trembling of his huge, hard body against her betrayed his massive effort to retain his self-control.

Parisa arched off the bed, her heart stopping as shudders of ecstasy rippled through her. Her fingers dug into his taut buttocks, her long legs thrashing wildly. The pleasure was too much, almost pain. 'Luc . . .' She whimpered his name, and, as though it was the sign he had been waiting for, he gathered her to him and drove into her, thrusting deep into her innermost core, claiming her completely.

He reared up on his hands, their bodies still joined, and stared into her flushed, love-swollen features. 'I want to watch you; I want to see what my body does to you,' he rasped, holding her pinned beneath him. Then slowly he began to move with strong, pounding strokes, his eyes wild, the pupils dilated to glittering black orbs of frenzied passion.

Parisa, her own eyes reflecting the same unbridled passion, reached out to Luc. Her skin burnt, her body was on fire, and she closed her eyes, as Luc increased the pressure, delving yet deeper, filling her so totally that she didn't think she could bear any more. But she was wrong, as Luc moved, plunging to a faster rhythm which her own body instinctively matched. She wound her long legs around his waist, clinging tighter. The tension inside her stretched to screaming pitch; she was sure she must die from the pleasure. Then she did scream—a long, keening yell, as spasm after spasm convulsed her in shattering pleasure. Her arms wrapped around his massive shoulders, her nails clawing at his smooth flesh, as his hard, sweat-slicked frame shuddered in a violent climactic response.

They were lying, bodies still joined in the afterglow of rapture. Parisa slowly dropped her arms to the bed as the glory faded and sanity returned. She squeezed her eyes tightly shut against the glaring electric light. She had not even had the benefit of darkness to hide her wanton behaviour. A tear trickled down her cheek, but it went unnoticed by Luc who, with a self-satisfied groan, rolled off her.

Furtively she wiped her cheek, and turned on her side away from him. She grasped the edge of the cover and made an ineffectual attempt to pull it over her throbbing nakedness.

Luc forestalled her, as his hand reached out over her shoulder to grab the cover and push it back. He swept the tangled mass of her hair to one side and, his mouth warm and firm, brushed a kiss against the side of her neck. His arm circled her waist and pulled her around to face him.

Parisa was trapped by the quivering sensations which her body welcomed but her head despised. She stared up into his darkly flushed face. He was supporting his weight on one elbow, and with his other hand he gently flicked the hair from her forehead.

'So, Parisa, are you willing to admit the truth?' he demanded huskily. 'There was never any question of force between you and I. I only have to touch you and the chemical reaction between us is as explosive as ever.

You are one electric lady in bed. You're everything a man could want,' he added, his sensuous mouth quirking at the corners in a wicked smile.

Parisa, her body sated, but her emotions torn to shreds, hated him at that moment. 'My body might want you, but in my heart I despise you——'

'I have no interest in the female heart; it is remarkably fickle. Your body will do very nicely, thank you very much...' he drawled cynically.

He was a heartless swine. Parisa had always known that, but the pain that knifed through her breast at his words left her feeling raw, and used. Helplessly aware of his warm, damp flesh hard against her, she forced herself to hold his gaze. Not by a single flicker of emotion would she reveal how much he had hurt her. Her pride wouldn't allow it.

'You do surprise me. As I remember, you seemed to think I was less than pleasing the last time,' she prompted. She hadn't forgotten his taunt.

'I must have been mistaken, or perhaps, like a fine wine, you improve with age,' he mocked throatily. 'I'd better have another sip; just to make sure, you understand...' His dark head bent towards her.

'Oh, God! No,' she groaned, trying to push him away, but his lips, surprisingly gentle, teased and nibbled at her mouth with devastating effect, until he eased her on to her back, one long leg nudged between her thighs, and she felt the stirring of his renewed arousal. She tried to stop the shiver of awareness that made her body quiver in anticipation, but, as if sensing her brief resistance, he deepened the kiss, his tongue darting between her teeth in a probing game of seduction.

Not again, her mind screamed, but her trembling body had a will of its own that was much more powerful. Her small hands stopped pushing him away, and instead stroked up to his wide shoulders.

Luc raised his head when he felt her capitulation. His smouldering eyes fixed on her swollen breasts, and his hand trailed over the luscious mounds and lower, to her stomach, tracing her feminine contours with a tactile delight. His fingers stroked her gently, intimately, down to the soft brush of pale hair. Her hips arched towards him, her body once more ablaze with need.

'A natural blonde. All cool and ice on the outside——' his voice was low and husky with desire '— and all fire and passion within.' He crushed her beneath his own taut and ready body.

Parisa did not even attempt to deny him. She was defeated, drowning in a violent torrent of emotions she could not control. Their bodies fused together as though they were made for each other, pale skin against golden brown. Wet with sweat, musky with the scent of love, they writhed in a primitive pagan rhythm, hands and mouths, clinging bodies straining for the ultimate climax. Until finally they lay drained and sated, in a tangle of limbs.

'I'm not sure I can last two weeks,' Luc groaned some time later, and, rolling over her, he pushed back the covers, and then rolled back, taking her pliant body with him. Gently he pulled the covers over them.

Parisa only vaguely registered his words, her eyes closed, and she made no demur when Luc put a possessive arm around her waist and tucked her into the hard warmth of his huge body. She was asleep...

She was unaware of the large man, wide awake, feasting his eyes on her sleeping form, and, when she stirred slightly, carefully tucking the satin sheet around under her chin, or of the gentle kiss he placed on her soft cheek, before reaching out and switching off the light, closing his eyes, and burying his face in the soft, sweet fragrance of her silver-blonde hair. His whispered 'My moon goddess' went unheard in the silence of the night.

Parisa woke up slowly. At first she did not know where she was; she was only conscious of feeling wonderfully warm and safe. Then suddenly reality returned. Luc's long arm encircled her waist. She moved slightly, edging away from him, and he turned, groaning in his sleep, to lie with his back to her.

She couldn't believe the enormity of what she had done. She lay on her back and stared at the ceiling as the morning light darted through the window. She watched the motes of dust dancing in the spring sunshine, and seriously considered flight as she despaired over her folly of the previous night. But she quickly dismissed the notion. She had made a deal, and she had to stick to it. It was her own idiotic fault that she had ended up in bed with Luc.

The deep, even sound of his breathing was the only noise in the room. He hadn't lied to her. Devious, a lie by omission, maybe. He must have known full well that she had thought he meant a platonic marriage of convenience. God knew that he read her mind easily enough at any other time, she thought angrily. Too well...

Resentment burned within her. His expertise as a lover was not in doubt: last night had proved that. She had surrendered to his masterful passion with humiliating ease. She cringed inwardly at the thought of her wanton response to his lovemaking. Her mind reeled with one crazy thought after another. Dear heaven! How was she going to survive the next fortnight? But more terrifying was how would she survive the rest of her life without him?

Parisa had told herself over and over again that she didn't love Luc, that it had been a mental aberration, that was all. But now, lying naked in bed with him, the heat of him reaching out to her, the musky scent of him lingering on the air she breathed, she finally admitted it. She had lied to herself, surely the very worst kind of lie... She had agreed to his business proposition, when perhaps, deep in her subconscious...had she been hoping to end up in his arms again?

She had been bitter and disillusioned when he had not contacted her on her return to London, determined to block him out of her mind, but now she was forced to readjust her thinking. She still loved him... Luc was a user and a taker, ruthless in the pursuit of what he wanted, the gratification of his own desire his main aim. How could she love him? But, deep down, a little voice whispered. He was not entirely selfish as a lover. He certainly gratified all Parisa's desire; he had the power to take her to the heights and beyond.

She turned her head to look at the object of her chaotic thoughts. His short-cropped hair was just beginning to grow. Then she gasped. Instinctively she lifted her hand, and reached out to touch the long, jagged scar that gouged a line from the edge of Luc's hairline down his neck. It was red and obviously quite new. She traced the shape with her finger; it was like a half-moon.

Steely fingers grasped her wrist as Luc spun around, wide awake. 'What's the matter, Parisa? Does my scar upset you?' he demanded icily.

'No, no, of course not,' she replied quickly, wondering at his obvious anger. 'I had never noticed it before,' she offered, suddenly acutely aware of his nakedness, his long legs brushing lightly against her, and the threatening look on his unshaven face.

She felt herself blush scarlet, the events of last night uppermost in her mind. 'What happened?' she queried quickly, hoping he wouldn't notice her blush.

He arched one eyebrow. 'Do you really want to know?' he asked sardonically.

'Yes.' If she kept him talking, it might keep his mind off the intimacy of the bed.

He let go of her wrist, and lay down on his back, not looking at her. 'The day after the fire at the factory, I went around the burnt-out building with the insurance assessor. Unfortunately the fabric of the building was unsafe. A roof joist fell and caught me on the back of the head.'

'Oh, my God!' Parisa sat up in bed, and stared down into his impassive face. He'd been hurt, and she hadn't known.

'Yes. I spent a week in a coma, and a few more weeks convalescing.'

She was completely unconscious of how desirable she looked, naked to the waist, her gorgeous hair a tangled mass around her shoulders. So that was why he hadn't called her. He couldn't; he had been ill. The information put an entirely different complexion on their relationship, she recognised immediately. Her full lips parted in a wide, beautiful smile, her heart lifting. 'You would have called me.' He hadn't used her as she had thought. But Luc was not smiling.

'Yes, I probably would have called sooner, but under the circumstances it is just as well I didn't—you obviously weren't that concerned. This way we have no illusions about each other.'

Parisa didn't understand. 'You weren't concerned', he had said. But she hadn't known. Her smooth brow creased in a frown. If she had, she would have dashed to his bedside. She stretched out her hand and brushed the short dark hair on his head. 'Your hair... that's why you had it cut,' she murmured softly, her blue eyes wide and tender.

'Of course.' He pulled his head back out of her reach, his face shuttered and blank. 'I wouldn't willingly walk around half scalped.' And, swinging his long legs off the bed, he rose to his full height, stretched his arms above his head, then casually picked his towelling robe from a nearby chair, and shrugged into it, before turning to glance at Parisa. 'I'll order coffee, then shower. Take your time—you look tired,' he said hardly and, collecting an assortment of clothes from the wardrobe, he walked out of the room.

Parisa opened her mouth to speak, but the words wouldn't come. What could she say? I waited for your call, and when it didn't come decided you were a bastard and hated you. That would certainly go down well! She had told him she despised him, acted like a mercenary gold-digger, agreeing to his proposal. How could she now declare she loved him?

She fell back on the bed, the shock of her discovery and what it implied almost too much to assimilate. She had a horrible sinking sensation in her heart, and a slowly growing conviction that she had made yet another mistake. She should have had more faith in him originally, instead of worrying over the fact that she thought he was a liar and a crook. At the very least, when she discovered on the Sunday his true identity she should have tried to contact him, then perhaps their relationship would have grown in a normal way. Instead she had run home to lick her wounds, hating him, and all the time he had been ill.

How had she never noticed the scar before? But then she realised that when he had first reappeared in her life he had worn a white roll-neck sweater, and, of course, the Cossack shirt at the hospital the next day. It made sense: the clothes disguised his injury.

Tears misted her lovely eyes. How he must have suffered. Injured himself, and then having to deal with his mother's illness. No wonder he had looked gaunt and thin. Why hadn't she realised? she asked herself over and over again. She brushed the tears from her cheeks with the back of her hand. God, but she was insensitive! she castigated herself. So wrapped up in her own selfish problems that she had never considered that there could be a valid reason for Luc's lack of communication.

But what was she going to do about it? And would it change anything? He had said 'This way we have no illusions about each other.' Perhaps she was being foolish all over again? The simple fact of admitting she did not know he was hurt was not going to make him love her.

The stark reality of her situation struck her a body blow. Any time in the past few days Luc could have mentioned his accident. The night at dinner, when he had hit his head. She had actually asked him if he was ill, and he had denied it. Once again she was falling into the trap of weaving her dreams around Luc.

She sat up in the large bed. She had to get a mental grip on herself. Wondering, What if? was not going to do her any good at all. Luc wanted her body; he had proved that last night. Just thinking about it made her toes curl. But he had also told her he wasn't interested in her heart. Maybe, just maybe, she could make him change his mind, she thought resolutely, and, jumping out of bed, a new determination in her step, she entered the bathroom.

Standing under the steaming spray of the shower, she made her decision. She would tell Luc she had not known about his accident, and how sorry she was, and let him draw his own conclusion. She loved and wanted him. Maybe propinquity and a willing woman in his bed might persuade him to alter their limited marriage into a lifelong commitment. She could but try...

Ten minutes later Parisa, dressed in her favourite straight blue tweed skirt and matching blue sweater, her long hair swept back and tied with a silk scarf, and wearing a minimum of make-up, walked into the living area of the suite.

Luc was sitting at the small dining table, a sheaf of papers in front of him, and a coffee-pot with the accompanying cups. He glanced up as she entered.

'No bacon and eggs today?' she said lightly to hide her nervousness.

'It's Easter Friday—the one day of the year I fast until after church.' His black eyes casually flickered over her. 'You can come with me, then we'll have lunch and visit Mother.' He laid out his plan for the day with barely a glance at Parisa, his attention once more on the documents in front of him.

Parisa sat down opposite him and helped herself to a cup of coffee. Greedily she drank it, the strong, hot brew reviving her flagging confidence. She looked at his downbent head, and ached to reach out and touch him. Instead she curled her hands around the now empty cup, and, keeping her eyes lowered to the tablecloth, she said softly, 'Luc, I never knew you were ill. If I had, I would have tried to get in touch with you. I'm sorry.'

He lifted his head, and studied her pale face. 'Yes, I'm sure you would,' he said drily. 'Tell me, do you still keep in touch with your friend Moya?'

Parisa couldn't credit his reaction. It meant nothing to him, her declaration and apology. Instead he was questioning her about her friend. She lowered her lashes to hide the hurt she knew must be revealed in her eyes. She had her answer to all her earlier heart-searching. Luc didn't care... But she couldn't quite believe it. She had to try again. 'Yes, of course. But Luc, about your accident. I——'

'Forget it, Parisa.' He stood up and, walking around to where she sat, he bent and pressed a kiss to the top of her head, before taking her arm and urging her to her feet.

She stood in front of him, her eyes drinking in his tall body, immaculately dressed in a dark three-piece suit and white silk shirt, a plain dark blue silk tie knotted neatly at his throat. She tilted her head back to look up into his handsome face, and their eyes locked. 'Luc——' she began, but he cut her off. His arms enfolding her, his lips found hers in a long, strangely tender kiss. She was trembling when he finally broke the kiss and held her away from him, his strong hands firmly clasping her upper arms.

'The past is over and finished with, Parisa. You are my wife, and I don't think you found last night too unpleasant. In fact, you were with me all the way.' His dark eyes bored down into hers, daring her to deny it.

'Yes,' she confessed with a shy smile.

'Good. So no more arguing and no more dragging up the past, and I think we will get through the next couple of weeks famously.'

Parisa wanted to touch him, wanted to love him, but instead she took the two weeks he was offering. 'That's fine by me,' she agreed, while vowing to try and make the fortnight into a lifetime.

Luc curved his arm around her shoulders and, tilting her chin with one finger, placed a swift, soft kiss on her full lips. 'Go and get your coat,' he said and, turning her around, he patted her bottom with a proprietorial hand. 'And hurry up, wife. I'm starving, and it's not good for my system to restrain my appetite...' His seductive chuckle echoed in her ears as she walked back into the bedroom.

Naked, spread-eagled on top of Luc, Parisa groaned. 'God! I'm shattered—utterly and completely shattered.' A deep masculine chuckle disturbed the tendrils of her hair spread over his chest...

'You are also shameless, my sweet wife.'

Parisa reared up, resting her folded arms on his massive chest, and stared down into his ruggedly attractive face. 'I am?' she jeered. 'And who was it who dragged me out of the cocktail bar and into the lift with indecent haste to have his evil way with me?' she teased him, plopping a soft, wet kiss on his invitingly curved lips. The past two weeks had been a revelation to Parisa. She had never imagined making love could be so varied and so ecstatic. She wriggled slightly. Her stomach felt as though it were glued to Luc's naked flesh, and she loved the feeling.

'No, you don't, *cara*.' Luc declared throatily and, wrapping her up in his arms, he got to his feet. They had never made it past the living-room floor, the urgency of their passion overcoming common sense. 'It's almost visiting time,' he said as he carried her naked into the bedroom and dropped her on the wide bed.

She laughed up at him, her blue eyes sparkling. 'It's not me who has the gargantuan appetite.'

'Maybe not for food, but in every other respect you match me, Parisa,' Luc said with a grin, then, brushing her hair from her brow, he sat on the side of the bed. 'Why don't you spend the next couple of hours cosseting this beautiful body of yours?' His strong tanned hand slid lazily over her pouting breast and down the length of her pale body with a proprietary pleasure. 'I'll go to the hospital myself, and later, when I return, wear something stunning. I'm taking you out.'

Languorously she smiled up at him, her flesh tingling from his soft caress. 'Yes, oh, lord and master,' she teased.

'I mean it, Parisa,' Luc said, suddenly serious. 'Mother was supposed to be released today. As you know, it was postponed, but I spoke to the consultant earlier, and now it's been decided she can leave for Italy tomorrow. So you and I have some talking to do.' And, getting up from the bed, he added, 'I won't be long—a couple of hours at most.'

Parisa hugged herself as he vanished into the bathroom. Maybe, just maybe, things would work out as she wanted them to. She loved Luc with all her heart, and the past two weeks had only served to deepen her feelings, if that were possible. From the first day of their marriage she had been living in a sensual dream. Luc was a masterful lover, with an insatiable appetite that she matched perfectly. They were highly compatible. No—combustible, more like, she thought with a secret smile. He only had to look at her a certain way and she knew exactly what he was thinking. They made love morning, noon, and night. Mostly in bed, but, like this evening, quite often not making it that far.

They were lovers, but out of bed there was still an indefinable barrier between them. She told herself it was because of his mother, but she was not convinced that was all. This afternoon they had stopped for a drink downstairs, and, not for the first time, he had abruptly, almost angrily demanded she go upstairs with him. She sighed. It had ended wonderfully—it always did—but she wished she knew what he was thinking, how he really felt. Now, he said he wanted to talk, and she hoped with all her heart that it was because he wanted to continue with their marriage.

Luc strolled back into the room, and avidly Parisa watched him as he moved from the drawers to the wardrobe, pulling on his clothes. Even the simple act of dressing he managed to do with an erotic grace, she thought, unable to take her eyes off him.

'See you later, *cara*.' And, bending down, he gave her a swift kiss. 'And hold that look until I return.' His lips quirked in a wide, natural smile as he left.

Parisa spent the next hour happily doing as he had instructed. The only cloud on the horizon was the fact that Luc had never mentioned the two-week deadline on their marriage, and she didn't dare...

CHAPTER TEN

PARISA stepped out of the bath, and, pulling on Luc's robe, she wrapped her long hair in a towel and eyed her glowing reflection in the bathroom mirror. A knock on the door interrupted her toilet. Luc back already? She smiled. Tying the belt of her robe firmly around her waist, she rushed through the suite and opened the door.

She stared at the woman in the doorway, one hand gripping the door-handle in a death grip, her knuckles white with the strain, as all the air seemed to vacate her lungs in one dizzying rush. Margot Mey!

'Oh, I'm sorry, you're still here. How silly of me,' she gushed. 'I could have sworn Luc told me on Monday you were leaving Thursday. You don't mind if I come in, do you?' And Parisa, her hand dropping from the handle, gestured Margot inside, trying desperately to gather her scattered wits together. 'Is Luc around? If not I'll nip into his office and leave a note. I just couldn't wait to thank him for the beautiful bracelet.' And, stretching out a slender arm, she displayed a sparkling diamond-studded strap around her slender wrist. 'He is such a darling and so generous. But then, of course, you must know that.' She laughed. The high tinkling tone sounded like a death knell in Parisa's stunned brain.

Parisa silently welcomed the icy numbness that engulfed her. It gave her the strength to say with chilling politeness, 'Please help yourself. I'm sure you know the way, but if you will excuse me I have my packing to finish.' On leaden feet she walked into the master bedroom, and closed the door behind her.

Dear God! Was there no end to her stupidity? 'Monday' Margot had said. On that day Luc had insisted he had a lot of work to catch up on, and suggested Parisa return to Hardcourt Manor for a few hours and check up on the redecoration. Now she knew his real reason. He had arranged to meet his mistress! How could she have forgotten so completely his long-standing affair with Margot Mey? Her gaze settled on the large bed, and she shuddered. She had slept with him in the same bed he had shared with Margot and God knew how many more... A humourless smile twisted her beautiful mouth. Poor Luc—his superb efficiency had finally let him down. His mother's departure delayed a day, and he was left with two women for the night, instead of one...

Grateful for the frozen state of her emotions, she methodically moved around the large room. Shedding her robe, she pulled on a simple wool dress. The row of designer clothes hanging in the wardrobe, which Luc had enthusiastically chosen for her on numerous shopping sprees, she ignored. Only packing the few clothes she had arrived with in her own suitcase, she walked out of the bedroom.

She glanced around the sitting-room. There was no sign of Miss Mey, but her attention was caught by a lipstick lying on the mantlepiece. She picked it up. Margot's! It was a deep dark red, and defiantly she scrawled on the mirror above, 'Deal concluded. Parisa.'

Exactly two weeks to the day from her arrival she walked out of the hotel, hailed a taxi, and climbed in. The numbness that had supported her for the past half-hour eased away, and a wrenching pain forced her to clutch her stomach, her eyes squeezed tightly shut.

Parisa grimaced as she stopped her old car outside the manor house. She sat for a moment, balefully eyeing the mass of scaffolding surrounding her home. The foreman had assured her the new roof would be finished this weekend. Personally, she no longer cared. She was bone-deep tired. Two days spent camping and teaching white-water canoeing to the Seventh Battle scout troop of which David was captain had done little to improve her state of health. David had behaved like a sulky schoolboy himself, letting her know he considered she had treated him very badly. There was nothing much she could say in her own defence, because he was right. She knew she had behaved less than honourably towards him.

Wearily she slid out of the car and reluctantly entered the house. The changes were immediately obvious. The wood parquet floor of the hall had been scraped, sealed and polished, the cornice and ceiling all repainted. A new stair carpet held in place with brass runners enhanced the grand staircase. The only jarring effect was the absence of the family portraits, revealing lighter patches on the mellow oak panelling of the walls. They had been removed for cleaning.

In the three weeks since she had walked out of the hotel and Luc's life, the alterations in her home had proceeded with break-neck efficiency. Didi was ecstatic about the new kitchen and the new bathrooms. At the moment the plumber was installing a bathroom in the new master suite. Parisa had decided on the design and colour scheme when in London with Luc. Now she could not bear to go near the room. In fact she was fast reaching the stage where she had to force herself to walk into her old home at all.

She dropped her rucksack in the hall, her hand going to undo the tie at her neck, then pulling off the scarf restraining her hair. She must get out of her uniform, she thought tiredly. She would give anything for a good night's sleep, but knew all the money in the world could not bring her the peace of mind she craved.

'Good, you're back, Miss Parisa. I thought I heard something.' Didi stood at the foot of the stairs.

'Yes, Didi, and I'm going to have a bath and an early night. I have school tomorrow.'

'But it's only five, and what about dinner? I've made all your favourites.'

Parisa stopped, one foot on the stair, and, turning her head, she looked at the older woman. She knew she had hurt Didi deeply by refusing point-blank to discuss her marriage, and she did not want to hurt her any more, but the last thing she needed after canoeing with a horde of kids all weekend was to have to face yet more signs of her new wealth in the form of an expensively refurbished dining-room. 'Please, Didi. I'm shattered.'

'And what am I supposed to do with the food I have already cooked?'

'All right, give me an hour or so.' Parisa relented, and, turning, began to ascend the stairs. The deep pile carpet was rich beneath her feet, but her lips curled with distaste as she reached the upper hall. How had she ever convinced herself she was cynical enough to sell herself for the sake of a house? She must have had a brainstorm. There was no other explanation. It hurt her every time she looked at all the alterations, knowing who had paid for them ... She closed her bedroom door behind her with a heartfelt sigh of relief.

Her sanctuary: the one place not yet altered. She eyed her old four-poster bed longingly, but forced herself to strip off her uniform and, slipping on her robe, made her way to the bathroom. After a quick shower she returned to her room, and, still wearing only her robe, gratefully lay down on the old bed. At least here there was nothing to remind her of her folly, she thought, and closed her eyes.

She was immediately tormented by images of Luc and the passion she had found in his arms, the naïve hope she had felt that he would fall in love with her, and the terrible night when all her hopes and dreams were so brutally betrayed. She relived in her mind the journey from the hotel.

She had left the taxi at the railway station and dashed for the ladies' room, where she had been violently sick. She had had no idea how long she had sat there until a railway official had told her they were locking up for the night. The last train had left. She had spent the night lying on a single bed in a seedy hotel, crying her eyes out. The following morning, when she had returned to Hardcourt Manor, Didi had greeted her in extreme agitation. Luc had called countless times. Parisa had walked past the exasperated Didi, refusing to discuss him, or ring the number he had left.

She never wanted to hear from the lying swine again. The following day, the clothes she had left behind arrived by post, and any lingering subconscious hope that Luc might care for her was squashed for all time. The note that accompanied the clothes read: 'You earned them, keep them. Luc.'

Parisa sighed, and finally slid into an uneasy sleep. Oh, God! It was happening again. Would this dream never cease? She felt the flood of heat in her slender body, and stirred restlessly on the wide bed. His lips, so firm, so smooth, so hot, were once again trailing across her skin, down the curve of her cheek, teasing the corner of her mouth. Her lips parted, but the heated caress travelled on down her throat. She moaned softly, her eyelashes fluttering. She wanted to lose herself in the dream, but knew the agony of waking up alone and frustrated was too much to bear.

Parisa forced her eyes open, and gasped. It was no dream. Sitting on the side of the bed, leaning over her, one hand either side of her shoulders, was Luc. 'You . . .' she exclaimed.

'I should hope so. Who else but your husband has the right to be in your bedroom?' his mocking voice demanded.

'How did you...? Who let you in?' she asked hoarsely, her pale face flooding with colour.

She watched as he rose from the bed and walked across to the window, his back to her. His hair had grown—progressed from short and spiky to soft curls. She could see the beginning of the savage scar on the back of his neck before it was hidden beneath the cream collar of his knitted shirt. His broad shoulders seemed oddly tense. Her eyes slid down the long length of him—his taut buttocks, the muscular legs covered in dark tan trousers. She couldn't tear her gaze away. Once she had known his body as intimately as her own. The heat scorched through her as a vivid mental image of her and Luc naked... Brutally she stamped down on the image, and sat up. Readjusting her robe more firmly around her, she swung her legs to the floor. The silence was filled with an electric tension that she was desperate to dispel.

'What are you doing here?' she demanded coolly, amazed at the even timbre of her voice, when in reality she felt as though she were dying inside.

'It's not unusual for a man to want to see his wife.' Luc turned and sat down on the wide window-sill, one long leg stretched negligently in front of him, the other hooked sideways across the sill. The fabric of his trousers pulled tight across his thigh, his elegantly shod foot swinging back and forwards, the muscles in his thigh rippling erotically with the movement, and Parisa swallowed hard as an unwanted stab of desire pierced her loins.

'In the ordinary course of events, yes, but surely that does not apply in our case?' She arched one delicate eyebrow in mock query, and bravely faced him. The evening sun behind him tipped his black hair with gold. His rugged features were remarkably bland, but for some reason his dark eyes avoided her direct stare. If she had not known better she could have sworn he looked unsure, almost wary. But Luc Di Maggi had never had a moment's uncertainty in his life. He knew what he wanted and took it, as she knew all too well.

'"Our case",' he parroted. 'Which reminds me, did you have a good weekend?'

'Strenuous, but good fun.' She wondered how he knew and couldn't resist asking.

'I rang on Saturday morning. Didi told me you had left for the weekend. It is rather a humiliating experience to be told by the housekeeper where one's wife is and who with. David, wasn't it?' he sneered and straightened up, his black eyes seeking hers as he continued, 'Your old boyfriend.'

Her blue eyes widened in astonishment. There was nothing unsure about him. He looked furious, but what had he said? Didi had spoken to him.

'Was he good, Parisa? Did he make you cry out the way I can?' he demanded icily, advancing towards her with an ominous expression on his rugged face. 'Did you wrap this glorious silver hair around him?' His hand snaked out and caught a handful of her long hair, tugging her towards him, the icy anger in his tone giving way to something much more sinister... 'Did you cling and whimper his name? Did you? You bitch...'

'What's it got to do with you?' she bit out, her hands pushing against his massive chest, as she looked a long way up into his furious black eyes. 'You and I had a deal, and it's finished.' How dared he call her names, assume she was as immoral as he was, the swine? She had wept buckets for this man. What a waste of emotion...

He went oddly white round the mouth. '*Dio*, Parisa. Don't try me too far or I'll make you regret it.'

A bitter smile contorted her full lips. As for regret, she already rued the day she had ever met him. 'And you have a lot further to go, so I suggest you leave now...' she said sarcastically while battling to subdue the wayward feelings his closeness aroused in her traitorous body.

'No one, least of all you, my darling wife, gives me my marching orders,' he snarled, his voice deep and harsh. His mouth crushed down on hers in a savage, brutal assault. When he finally lifted his head to stare with hostile eyes into her flushed face, she was clinging to his broad shoulders, her robe gaping open, her body melded against his, to her shame once more a slave to his passion.

'This David of yours certainly didn't satisfy you, my insatiable little wanton,' Luc rasped savagely, and, lifting his hand, he stroked over the burgeoning fullness of her breast. 'You want me still, Parisa. I can see it in your eyes, so don't try to deny it.'

It was true; she did want him. She stilled in his arms, and forced herself to ignore the rising heat in her overwrought body. She took a step back, pushing him away, her blue eyes brilliant with sensuous arousal but, even more, with a fast growing, furious rage.

'No denial, Parisa,' he mocked, once more reaching for her.

The last slender thread of her self-control finally snapped as she looked up into his dark face and saw the smug, knowing gleam in his black eyes. She turned on him like a virago. 'You conceited, arrogant bastard!' She pushed him again in the chest, and, recovering once more, he reached out for her. But she avoided him. 'You call me a wanton! That's rich, coming from you. At least if I have a lover it's one at a time, but you... You couldn't stay true to one woman for two weeks.' Wildly she flung out her hand in a gesture of dismissal. '"You go down to Hardcourt, Parisa",' she parodied his voice. '"I have a lot of work", you said. Work! What a joke. Work on your mistress, Margot. Do you think I am a complete idiot? You're a raging bloody sex maniac. I'm an angel in comparison. And as for wanting you ... well, buster,

I have news for you. I'd see you in hell before I would
let you touch me again. Now get out...'

'You know about Margot?' he prompted, his
handsome face paling beneath his tan, his strong hands
dropping to his sides.

Parisa laughed, a harsh, cynical sound. 'I've known
about Margot Mey since before I ever met you again.'
Revenge was sweet, she thought furiously. 'When I
burgled your apartment I entered by the bathroom
window, not the door, and overheard you telling Miss
Mey you hadn't time. A first for you, no doubt,' she
couldn't resist observing mockingly. 'But you promised
to make it up to her later. I must say, Luc, you could
do with expanding your English. You used almost the
same words to me when you left me in Italy.' Her blue
eyes clashed with black and the anger she saw in his made
her sick. He was furious because he had been found out,
she thought bitterly. 'It only surprises me that your usual
superefficiency let you down at last, though, given your
appetite, no doubt two at a time would probably appeal
to you.'

Parisa spun around and headed for the door. Margot
had described Luc as a 'master of passion', and to
Parisa's shame, he *had* been where she was concerned.
But no more... She couldn't stand to look at the man
any longer. Remembering the last time she had seen him
was too painful. He had left her in bed, sated by his
loving, but with someone else lined up to take her place.
He had caused her nothing but pain and heartache from
the minute she had first laid eyes on him. She almost
made it out of the room...

'Wait, Parisa.' A strong arm curved around her waist,
lifting her from the floor.

'Let me go, you pig!' she spat.

'No, Parisa, please...'

She began fighting in earnest, but Luc was a very big
man, and with insulting ease he manhandled her to the

old four-poster bed and dropped her in the middle. Following her down, he grasped her wildly flaying arms and pinned them to her sides, while the pressure of his huge body held her a prisoner beneath him.

'You cannot fling accusations like that around and not give me a chance to repudiate them!'

'Why not? You do...' she sneered, still furious at his assumption that she had spent the weekend with a man.

'*Dio*! Parisa, what kind of a man do you think I am?' he demanded hoarsely. 'Do you honestly believe I have so little respect, so few morals that I would keep two women at the same time——?'

'Yes. Now let me up,' she said coldly. 'You and I have nothing more to say to each other.'

'Well, I have plenty to say to you, and you are not going anywhere until we have talked.' His handsome face was flushed and frowning. 'First I want to know what you meant by saying my usual efficiency had deserted me. You were talking about the last night at the hotel.' She watched him and could see his astute brain mulling over her words. 'What exactly happened after I left to visit Mother that made you run away?'

'What's the point?' Parisa turned her head to one side. She didn't want to face him, suddenly afraid she might have revealed more than she wanted him to know.

'Tell me; I demand to know,' he insisted. 'I left a willing woman in my bed and came back to an empty suite, and a lipstick scrawl on the mirror.'

'The colour of the lipstick should have told you,' she snapped.

'Bright red...' His hard body moved restlessly above hers. She could feel the heat from his long limbs burning into her, but was powerless to move. She could almost hear his brain ticking over.

'You never wear scarlet lipstick. Margot called at the hotel.'

'Got it in one.'

'You were jealous...'

Parisa stared up at him, and the devil was actually smiling. 'You're mad—stark, staring mad...' she told him bluntly.

'Yes, you're right, I am mad,' he agreed. His mouth twisted in a derisive smile. 'I suspect I've been slightly mad for years, and I know for a fact I've been crazy for the past few months. Crazily in love with a blue-eyed cat burglar.'

Parisa blinked. She was dreaming again; she had to be. She imagined she had heard Luc declare he loved her. But no, it wasn't a dream. She heard his shaky sigh as he rolled off her, and, swinging his legs to the floor, he sat up.

'Nothing to say, Parisa?' The silence was agonising, but she could not break it. She did not dare let down the precarious barrier she had built around her heart in the past few weeks. She was terrified of making a fool of herself yet again with this man. 'Why should you believe me?' he continued, and she was presented with his forceful profile, which revealed nothing. 'I've treated you abominably, and my only excuse is madness.' A harsh laugh escaped him. 'You were right in my anger and conceit when you ran away from the hotel. I packed up your clothes in a fit of rage, and thought, Let her stew for a couple of weeks. God knows! I spent two months agonising over you and in the end had to come and find you. But this time I've left it too late. You've found someone else, and all I can do is attack you like a madman.'

Parisa felt her heart swell with burgeoning hope. 'I've spent the weekend teaching white-water canoeing to the scout troop. David happens to be the captain, and at the minute he is barely speaking to me because I married you. I was in the tent with the girls, David with the boys,' she offered quietly.

His dark head jerked around and his black eyes sought hers. 'Canoeing? Scouting? God!' he said incredulously. 'I should have guessed. Didi told me you had gone away with David and you let me think you had been with him.'

'*I* did not have to think. You were with another woman—I met the lady,' Parisa said soberly.

Luc reached down and covered her hand where it lay on the bed, his fingers entwining with hers. 'I swear to you, Parisa, I have never looked at another woman from the day I threw you to the floor with a rugby tackle in the company apartment. I love you, and I came here today to convince you calmly and sensibly to give our marriage a chance, and also to kill you if what Didi told me on the telephone was true,' he said with wry self-mockery. 'The thought of any man touching you drives me mad with jealousy.'

Was this vulnerable man, her arrogant husband, truly jealous of her? She couldn't quite believe it, but oh, how she wanted to. 'I think Didi has been trying to do a little matchmaking. Whatever she said, you shouldn't believe her.' She pushed herself up and pulled her robe around her. Luc was sitting on the side of the bed but she couldn't look at him, as she added quietly, 'You never told me you cared.'

'Never told you...?' He laughed in self-derision. 'Oh, Parisa, every time we made love I told you over and over again. I poured out my heart to you in my native language.'

'Oh, Luc.' She swallowed hard. 'I didn't know.' He had always been a very verbal lover, but she had never understood what he was saying. 'I thought it was...was your mother and everything...' she muttered, hardly knowing what she was saying, as Luc put his arm around her shoulders, pulling her unresisting body into the curve of his side.

'Parisa, I am ashamed to confess I used my mother quite deliberately. Contrary to the impression I have given you over the past weeks, much as I love my mother, I rarely spend much time with her. She has her own apartment in Genoa, and her own circle of friends. She doesn't actually live with me. It was only for her birthday party she stayed at the villa, simply because it was big enough to accommodate all the guests. It was true she wanted me to settle down, but I have spent thirty-seven years avoiding any commitment, and I certainly would never have considered getting engaged solely to please *Mamma*.'

'But you said——' She wanted to believe him, but...

His hand tightened on her shoulder. 'Shh, Parisa, and listen. I have to say it all now before I lose my courage. I was smitten from the first time I lay on top of a certain lady dressed all in black and wearing a Balaclava, of all things, or perhaps before that, when a certain blue-eyed schoolgirl flirted outrageously with me. I don't know. I only know that when we met in the company apartment I wanted to see you again. When you started babbling about blackmail you gave me the ideal opportunity, and I couldn't resist the temptation of having you to myself for a few days. It was rotten of me to trick you, I know. But it was only when we had arrived in Italy and I was trying to seduce you in your bedroom and you were terrified and called me a blackmailer that the full realisation of my actions was brought home to me. I suddenly saw that in a way I was just as guilty as the original villain. That night over dinner when mother had pointed out how innocent you were, I felt a complete heel, and it wasn't a very good feeling. I knew then I loved you, and I wanted to confess everything, and persuade you to make our engagement real. I took you to the study with that thought in mind, but before I could get up the nerve we were arguing, then mother joined us for coffee.' Luc grinned. 'And it was too late.

'The following day we had so much fun I could not bring myself to spoil it by admitting my duplicity. I thought I had pienty of time; I had no intention of rushing you into a full relationship. Unfortunately I was hopelessly unprepared for the effect you have on my libido, and before I could control myself I was making love to you that very night. It never occurred to me that you could doubt how I felt about you. But when I had the accident and you never got in touch——'

'I didn't know. I waited in Moya's apartment for five days, for your call. I only left when it was time to return to work,' Parisa inserted.

'Yes, well, we won't go into that; it is over and done with,' Luc commanded, suddenly sounding quite harsh.

'But Luc——'

'Parisa, I'm not asking you to love me straight away. I know you don't feel the same. When I left the message on the answering machine at Moya's apartment I did think the least you could have done was respond.'

'What message?' she squeaked. 'I never——'

'Please, Parisa, don't bother with excuses. You told me yourself you shared her apartment and kept in touch with Moya. I rang ten days later, as soon as I could speak. She must have passed the message on.'

'Oh, Luc...' she sighed, burrowing closer to his male warmth. 'You're so wrong. I never received your call, and neither did Moya, I'm sure. She left London the same Sunday as I did. She went home to prepare for her wedding, and stayed there until going off on honeymoon. She isn't due back until tomorrow. I would have dashed straight to your side if I had known.'

'Oh, God, what a fool I've been,' Luc groaned. 'I was furious at what I saw as your heartless neglect. I lay in the hospital in Naples longing to hear the sound of your voice, and then, later, when I could travel, I was so furious you had not returned my call that I was going to come and see you and demand an explanation. But

Mother took ill. Then I saw my chance. I had to come to London and I went straight to the apartment and discovered from a neighbour that you had not even given me your own address. I was determined to find you again and make you pay for the heartache you'd caused me.'

It was ironic, Parisa thought, with a wry smile. Her one moment of caution in Italy, when she had given Luc Moya's phone number, was probably the main cause of all the heartache they had both suffered.

'It was sheer coincidence I discovered I owned the agency that was selling your title, and I couldn't believe my luck. Yours is an uncommon name and after a few discreet enquiries I realised I had found you. I bought the title hoping to use it to get at you, I freely admit.'

'Not because your mother had delusions of grandeur or something?'

'Are you crazy? Whatever gave you that idea?'

'Anna, in Italy. She said your mother wanted you to marry me as a kind of status symbol.'

'Rubbish. I'm six-four and filthy rich. I have all the status I need.' Luc smiled down at her. 'Now let me finish. As soon as I saw you again and realised your circumstances, I also realised I wanted you like hell. I was all you accused me of—devious and manipulative. But I thought once I got you back into my bed I would soon convince you to stay there.'

'You said I was no good in bed,' she reminded him, peeking up into his dark serious eyes.

'I lied, little cat.' His lips twisted in a wry smile. 'And you know it, but I had to have some defence against the terrible urge to fling you on the ground whenever I looked at you.'

Parisa sighed. This was where she belonged, wrapped in the warmth of Luc's arms, listening to his confession of love. She felt like pinching herself to make sure she had not died and gone to heaven. Instead she nuzzled into the curve of his shoulder.

'Stop that, Parisa. I haven't finished yet and I can't stand the distraction,' he murmured into her sweet-scented hair. 'I have so much to apologise for, and I will probably never have the courage to do this again. It is very sobering for a man like me to realise that just one flash from a particular pair of sapphire eyes, and I melt. I put the announcement of our engagement in the paper hoping to force you into accepting me. But when I saw you looking so beautiful and unconcerned I was furious and determined to make you pay for the trouble you had caused me.'

Now she knew why he had looked angry all the time.

'I could not resist once more manipulating you into my clutches. I told myself any woman who could desert her first lover because he had an accident was quite likely to be equally mercenary. So I decided to make a deal with you. I told myself it was to teach you a lesson, but I was only fooling myself. Deep down I was praying that after a couple of weeks with me you would not want to leave.'

'I never wanted to leave you.' She murmured the confession, but it was as though he never heard. Luc was too intent on his own confession.

'When we got married I thought I had succeeded. The last night, when I got back to the hotel anticipating taking you out for dinner and declaring my undying love, I was quietly confident you felt the same. I couldn't believe you had left me with a scrawled message on a mirror. I was frantic and furious. By the time I discovered the next morning that you had returned here it was too late to do anything about it. I had to accompany *Mamma* safely back to Italy. Also, the work had piled up in my absence...'

'You said before you thought "let her stew"...' she teased. 'And actually I am beginning to get rather hot.' She slipped her hand from his and curved it around his waist. She believed him. He was a proud, mature male, and there was no way he would lay his feelings on the line like this if he didn't really love her, she told herself.

She squeezed her eyes tight shut, so overcome with relief and love. He tilted her chin with one finger and wiped a tear from her cheek.

'Parisa, is there any hope for me? Will you give our marriage a chance? Forgive me, and let me try and make you love me . . .'

'I've loved you from the first night in Italy.' She smiled brilliantly up into his tender black eyes. 'But when you never called for five days, I had to return home. I told myself you had used me for sex, nothing more. I knew only days before you had seen Margot, and I heard you promising to spend the weekend with her, and then two days later it was me.'

'Parisa, Parisa.' He lifted her bodily on to his lap, his strong arms enfolding her, holding her close to his broad chest. 'You have to listen to me. I don't know what you overheard, but I can assure you I did not sleep with Margot that weekend. After I met you and realised my ex-manager was also a blackmailer I spent the rest of the weekend helping the police to capture him. I had not been with Margot for some months. It was only ever a casual affair. When I was in London she was a convenient partner. I'm not proud of the fact, but it is the truth, and I had already decided to end it. If you were listening you must have realised I had not even told her where I was staying.' Parisa remembered now: Margot had said she had got his address from the casino.

'I had come to London that day specifically to sort out the mess at the casino. The apartment was part of the deal and had been used by the casino manager. I had stood over him while he packed his bags and left, and was only waiting for Tina to arrive with some more documents I had requested, before leaving myself when Margot turned up. I admit I bought a bracelet at Cartier, the day before you and I went for the ring, and it was for Margot, but it was a goodbye present. Not very laudable, I know, but I found the type of women in my life before you expected that kind of thing. I never actually saw Margot. She pestered me with telephone calls, and the Monday was the last time I spoke to her. I had the bracelet delivered by special messenger, along with a note making it absolutely clear I loved my wife and had no intention of ever seeing her again.'

'A pay-off...' Parisa could believe that. Hadn't Anna, the day after the birthday, warned her that she might have the ring but she would end up with the bracelet like the rest of them? 'You paid Anna the same way.'

'Oh, God!' Luc groaned. 'You make me sound terrible, Parisa, and I suppose in a way it is true. I just never really thought about it. A present and goodbye was the sum total of my commitment to any woman until I met you.'

Winding her slender arms around his neck, she lifted her face, urging his head down towards her waiting lips. 'Just make sure you never ever buy me a bracelet,' she murmured against his lips. They kissed gently, tenderly, but gentleness quickly gave way to a hungry passion that left them both shaking with the force of their mutual desire.

Reluctantly Luc put her away from him and stood up, walking across the room. 'I vowed if I ever had another chance with you I would not touch you until we were properly married again in church.'

Parisa lay back on the old bed, not caring that her robe had fallen open, leaving a length of naked thigh exposed. 'Do I get no say in the matter?' she asked huskily.

He whipped around, his dark eyes widening on her long, luscious body splayed across the bed, her glorious silver-gilt hair spread across the pillow, and as though attached by an invisible thread he moved towards her. 'Some girl scout, Parisa. Is seducing males part of your teaching, or are you always this impulsive?' he teased, grinning down at her, but the slight tremor in his voice told her all she wanted to know.

'Not impulsive,' she denied huskily.

Luc laughed out loud. '*Dio*! Parisa, have you not realised yet?'

'Realised what?' she asked, stretching her hand out to him.

'You are as adventurous and impulsive as any one of your illustrious ancestors. It was the one thing I counted on in my pursuit of you.'

'I don't think I like that remark.' Did Luc know her better than she knew herself? she wondered.

Luc grinned, his dark eyes gleaming with tender indulgence. 'You've spent the weekend white-water canoeing. Dangerous, *cara*! But then, at fourteen you dressed up as a woman and seduced me—not the action of a cautious spirit. You got to the Olympics through hard work and ruined it because you fancied a try at pole vaulting.' His grin widened. 'You scaled a fire-escape and broke into an apartment, for a friend.' He chuckled. 'You swanned off to Italy with a man you hardly knew, convinced at the time he was a crook...' His chuckle turned into a sensuous smile. 'In the observatory you gave yourself to me completely, without inhibition.' He couldn't resist lowering his head and kissing her long and lovingly. 'You sold the title to the manor without a second thought.'

'Well, maybe I am a tiny bit reckless,' she admitted when she could get her breath back. 'But I'm responsible. I work. Oh!' She suddenly realised she couldn't just walk off into the sunset with Luc. She had commitments—more than most... 'I have to live here, Luc, and I do enjoy my work, and——'

'I know, Parisa. You're a strong, vibrant woman and I am going to have my work cut out keeping up with you. But don't worry—I have it all arranged. I am going to live here. *Dio*! The place is big enough, and there is nothing in the covenant that can prevent the master of the house having a study with a mainstream computer. As for your job, I would never ask you to give up work, but I would like you to be able to travel with me when necessary. You could work on a part-time basis. Start your own fitness clinic—or you could coach. As long as you love me, I don't care what you do.'

She was stunned by his thoughtfulness, but still one question had to be asked. 'You don't think I'm really mercenary, Luc?'

'I know you agreed to marry me when you hated me, but I always knew your main concern was for Didi and Joe. Never money.'

Curving her arms around his back, she urged him down to her. He understood her far too well, she thought. But she did not want to hear any more about her nature— reckless or otherwise. Parisa was much more interested in what her body was telling her.

'So I'm impulsive,' she finally admitted throatily. 'And you want me to travel with you.' And, sliding her hands up under his shirt, she added, 'Like this,' as her fingers found the heated warmth of his chest and slid down to the fastening of his trousers. They had a lot to talk over, but a lifetime to do it in, and right now Parisa had a much more urgent need.

'Oh, yes, Parisa, carry on.' Luc groaned. 'This kind of impulsive travelling I can stand for the rest of my life, lady...' Luc lay down beside her. 'It was a stupid vow, anyway,' he declared raspingly as he gathered her hard against him. 'You are going to stay with me, Parisa. Say it. Promise you will be my wife for now and always?' he asked her unsteadily.

Her heart was bursting with love for the huge man who with a few words revealed all his uncertainty and vulnerability. She raised luminous blue eyes to his. 'I love you, Luc.' He stopped her words with a kiss, and when she could breathe again she added teasingly, 'I'm not sure about the lord and master bit, though.'

'You still haven't realised yet, Parisa. I would give you the world if I could. I love you, and, contrary to what you imagine, I am not the least chauvinistic.'

'This from "the master of passion "...' she joked, watching him carefully, but there was not a flicker of recognition of the phrase in his dark eyes, just a delighted gleam of satisfaction.

'I hope I will always be the master of your passion, but I have no desire to lord it over you,' he quipped. 'I doubt if anyone could.' And, cuddling her close, he chuckled softly. 'My darling, scatty, impulsive Parisa. My Lady and my wife.'

POSTCARDS FROM EUROPE

HARLEQUIN PRESENTS®

Travel across Europe in 1994 with Harlequin Presents. Collect a new Postcards From Europe title each month!

Don't miss
VIKING MAGIC
by Angela Wells
Harlequin Presents #1691

Available in October, wherever Harlequin Presents books are sold.

HPPE10

Hi!

The last thing I expected—or needed— when I arrived in Copenhagen was a lecture. But that's what Rune Christensen proceeded to give me. He clearly blames me for the disappearance of my sister and his nephew. If only Rune wasn't so attractive.

Love, Gina

Where do you find hot Texas nights, smooth Texas charm and dangerously sexy cowboys?

Crystal Creek reverberates with the exciting rhythm of Texas.
Each story features the rugged individuals who live and love in
the Lone Star state.

"...Crystal Creek wonderfully evokes the hot days and steamy
nights of a small Texas community...impossible to put down until
the last page is turned."
—*Romantic Times*

Praise for Bethany Campbell's *The Thunder Rolls*

"Bethany Campbell takes the reader into the minds of her characters
so surely...one of the best Crystal Creek books so far. It will be
hard to top...."

—*Rendezvous*

"This is the *best* of the Crystal Creek series to date."
—*Affaire de Coeur*

Don't miss the next book in this exciting series. Look for
GENTLE ON MY MIND by BETHANY CAMPBELL

Available in October wherever Harlequin books are sold.

THE VENGEFUL GROOM
Sara Wood

Legend has it that those married in Eternity's
chapel are destined for a lifetime of happiness.
But happiness isn't what Giovanni wants from
marriage—it's revenge!

Ten years ago, Tina's testimony sent Gio to
prison—for a crime he didn't commit. *Now* he's
back in Eternity and looking for a bride. *Now*
Tina is about to learn just how ruthless and
disturbingly sensual Gio's brand of vengeance
can be.

THE VENGEFUL GROOM, available in
October from Harlequin Presents, is the fifth
book in Harlequin's new cross-line series,
WEDDINGS, INC. Be sure to look for
the sixth book, **EDGE OF ETERNITY,** by
Jasmine Cresswell (Harlequin Intrigue #298),
coming in November.

WED5

HARLEQUIN®

PRESENTS Plus

One brief encounter had disastrously altered their futures, leaving Antonia with deep psychological scars and Patrick accused of a horrific crime. Will the passion that exists between them be enough to heal their wounds?

Fler knows she's in for some serious heartache when she falls for Kyle Ranburn, the man who caused her daughter so much pain. But she has no idea how difficult it is to be torn by her love for the two of them.

Fall in love with Patrick and Kyle—Antonia and Fler do!

Watch for

Wounds of Passion by Charlotte Lamb
Harlequin Presents Plus #1687

and

Dark Mirror by Daphne Clair
Harlequin Presents Plus #1688

Harlequin Presents Plus
The best has just gotten better!

Available in October wherever Harlequin books are sold.

This September, discover the fun of falling in love with...

Harlequin is pleased to bring you this exciting new collection of three original short stories by bestselling authors!

ELISE TITLE
BARBARA BRETTON
LASS SMALL

LOVE AND LAUGHTER—sexy, romantic, fun stories guaranteed to tickle your funny bone and fuel your fantasies!

Available in September wherever
Harlequin books are sold.

◆ HARLEQUIN ®
®

MIRA™

The brightest star in women's fiction!

This October, reach for the stars and watch all your dreams come true with **MIRA BOOKS**.

HEATHER GRAHAM POZZESSERE
Slow Burn in October
An enthralling tale of murder and passion set against the dark and glittering world of Miami.

SANDRA BROWN
The Devil's Own in October
She made a deal with the devil...but she didn't bargain on losing her heart.

BARBARA BRETTON
Tomorrow & Always in November
Unlikely lovers from very different worlds...they had to cross time to find one another.

PENNY JORDAN
For Better For Worse in December
Three couples, three dreams—can they rekindle the love and passion that first brought them together?

The sky has no limit with **MIRA BOOKS**